THE STRANGLER

KILLERS AMONG BOOK ONE

S. E. GREEN

PRAISE FOR THE SERIES

"The ending literally left me with my mouth hanging open–not only was it shocking, it was more than a little gruesome and bloody. In a word, perfect." ~Crimespree Magazine

"Dark and disturbing–a high stakes thriller that offers a window into a terrifying world." ~Kami Garcia, #1 NYT Bestselling Author

"S. E. Green spares no one--unique, beautifully twisted, and rich in mystery." ~Jennifer L. Armentrout, #1 NYT Bestselling Author

"A zippy, gripping psychological drama." ~Kirkus Reviews

"With an engaging and complex main character and a plot twist you'll never see, Green's thrillers are to die for." ~RT Reviews

"Readers will be most fascinated by Lane herself, an

emotion-less machine whose small twinklings of humanity are awakened as the killer gets ever closer." ~Booklist

"Readers who relish a darkly twisted crime drama with a well-managed surprise ending will enjoy curling up with this one." ~BCCB

AUTHOR'S NOTE

Everyone has a dark side, and I certainly explore mine when I write Lane.

She is the 18-year-old daughter of the infamous serial killer, The Decapitator. Lane was first introduced in *Killer Instinct* as a conflicted 16-year-old with a dark side she couldn't explain.

Now she can explain it.

Now she knows what to do with it...

I love to hear from my readers! Don't hesitate to shoot me an email shannon@segreen.net. I try my very best to respond to every message. You can also sign up for my (non-annoying) newsletter at www.segreen.net to gain access to free books and inside information.

1

LIFE IS SUPPOSED to be pretty routine, right? You graduate high school, work a summer job at Patch and Paw, help out at home, you get back into stalking...

I now consider the people I stalk my new pals. One can never have too many pals.

"So how are things, Lane?" Victor, my step-dad, asks over dinner on a Tuesday night. Pork chop night. "Enjoying your last summer?"

"Yep." I don't know why people refer to the summer before college as the "last summer". What, I'm never going to have a summer again? I don't get it.

My sister, Daisy, dredges her roll across her plate. "When's Tommy coming back?"

Even though I'm not indifferent to that question, I still shrug. "Not sure."

The last time I saw him, I hopped on the back of his motorcycle after Dr. Issa's funeral. We went for a very long ride, hours in fact, and then he delivered me back home.

Dr. Issa...now there's a name I haven't thought of in a

while. My former boss and the first person to make me sexually aware. I used to think my thing for him was one-sided until I learned differently. The age difference mattered more to him than me, but that was Dr. Issa for you—caring, intelligent, handsome.

Dead. Killed by Catalina, my copycat.

"Have you guys texted at all?" Daisy asks, and it takes my brain a second to catch back up.

"A few times." Months have gone by since Tommy left, and yes we've texted a few times. He dropped out of college, took a hiatus from his job at Whole Foods, and decided to do a cross-country ride. If I had already graduated high school, I probably would have gone with him. Not that he asked, but a trip like that sounds way too inviting.

BE BACK IN A FEW DAYS. That was the last text I got from him. I ride by his apartment every couple of days to see if he's back, and no motorcycle yet.

Justin, my younger brother, crinkles his nose. "At camp today this kid fell and busted open his head. There was so much blood!"

Daisy cringes. "Gross."

I perk up. "How much blood?"

My whole family looks at me, and this is why I need to keep my thoughts to myself.

Victor changes the subject. "So, it surprised me to see you had signed up for freshmen orientation. Doesn't really seem like your thing."

It's not, but I'd like to think I've been making more "normal" decisions lately, and these three sitting around the table make that possible. Yes, I'd like to think life is pretty good.

I turn to Daisy, going on this whole normal thing. "So Cheer Camp's good?"

"Some of the girls annoy me." She shrugs one shoulder, looking more like me than I think I'm comfortable with. "I'm not even sure I want to cheer anymore."

Victor and I exchange a surprised glance. Daisy's going to be a junior and officially inducted into the Varsity Squad. Cheer and Varsity have driven her whole life. I don't know if she's growing up or just out of her previous life. I guess her maturing has to start somewhere. Though if I had to put my finger on it, it would be the moment our mother died.

Or rather the moment I killed her.

"Um," Justin wipes his mouth and lays his napkin aside. "Tomorrow is 'bring-your-mom-to-camp-day'. Who am I supposed to bring?"

For a couple of seconds, no one says a word, then Victor says, "I'll go."

Justin sighs. "That won't work because then who will go next week on 'bring-your-dad-to-camp-day'?"

Daisy waves her hand through the air, straightening in her chair. "I'll go." She jokingly narrows her eyes at Justin. "That is unless there's a 'bring-your-sister-to-camp-day'?"

Justin giggles. "No, there's not that."

Daisy nods. "Then I'll go with you tomorrow." She glances my direction, and I give her my best big-sister smile because maturing is definitely what she's doing.

"Cool," Justin says, just like that. If anyone should have issues out of all this, it should be my little brother. No mother, anger, rejection, abandonment. He could claim it all, but not Justin. He rolls with it and moves on.

I could take a lesson from him. They both get up then, taking dishes in, and chatting about tomorrow.

Victor looks across the table at me, his expression calm. "I wasn't sure it would happen, but we are definitely falling into place. We're going to be okay. I've got three awesome kids. No drama. Good life. And I've finally figured out, it's okay to drop the ball. To relax. To rely on others. Things don't have to be perfect. Just okay. As long as I try my best, it's okay."

Yep, that's right. Rely on others.

Like me.

I'll make sure things are running smoothly. Like with old Ted Lowman, AKA "Teddy Bear". He first came to my attention in Judge Penn's court, where I like to spend some of my free time.

Teddy Bear killed a local high school girl and then was released on some sort of police mishandling of evidence, whereupon he falls off the radar.

Everyone's radar but mine.

2

LANE, THE MUFFIN girl. Part of my new thing. I show up at the start of every week to Patch and Paw with a box of muffins. The receptionist always takes blueberry. The groomer, a carrot walnut. The office manager, a chocolate chip. The janitor, a vanilla pear.

"Mm," the kennel assistant bites into her apple-cinnamon one. "Better than oral."

(A) I wouldn't know and (B) that's just too much information. I turn away, giving the last one, a double espresso, to Dr. Issa's replacement, Dr. O'Neal. She's nice, I guess, but she's no Dr. Issa. Still, I hand the muffin over with a little smile.

"Got a little favor," Dr. O'Neal says, grinning.

I hate that grin. It's always followed by some menial request. "Yes?"

"Bo-Bee is here, and you know how hard his anal glands are to express. You seem to be the only one he'll allow near his rear." She pinches off a delicate corner of the muffin and plunks it into her mouth. "Mind tackling that this morning?"

If Dr. Issa was here, I'd be assisting with surgery, but okay, whatever. "Sure."

Dr. O'Neal's grin gets bigger, and I really want to tell her she has a chunk of espresso bean stuck in her side tooth, but I refrain.

"Thanks!" She chirps, whirling away, before spinning right back. "By the way, love your new hair. Makes you look so mature."

Mature was not what I was going for. My kinky red hair used to hang down my back as it has pretty much my entire life, and now it's shoulder length for functional reasons only. It fits better up inside my neoprene full face mask.

In my back pocket, my phone buzzes and I check the display. I'M MEETING HAMMOND LATER. This is the text I get from Daisy.

OKAY, I text back. Hammond's her several-months-now boyfriend, and I have no clue why she's texting me. It's not like she needs my approval.

I THINK HE WANTS TO HAVE SEX. This is the next text to come in and total news to me. When they started dating, Hammond was adamant on the abstinence and no partying thing, and Daisy surprised me by jumping quickly on board. She hasn't been a virgin for a very long time and really sex has never been a hang up for her. Neither has partying. So I'm not really getting this.

AND? I text back.

I DON'T WANT TO, she quickly responds.

THEN DON'T, I type back.

OKAY, THEN I WON'T.

I think Daisy did the whole sex and partying thing because she was bored. She never really seemed to like it. It's almost like she thought it was a chore. Or a game. Or something she was supposed to do, like a show she needed to put on. I'm glad she's making her own decisions now and not feeling pressured to be someone she doesn't want to be.

My cell buzzes again with another text from my sister. YOU GOING TO BE HOME TONIGHT?

I DON'T KNOW, MAYBE.

WHY, she types back. WHERE ELSE WOULD YOU BE?

OUT, I quickly respond. Daisy sometimes gets a little too question-y when it comes to my personal life. I love who she's becoming and want her happy, but sometimes she crowds me.

MAYBE YOU FORGOT WE'RE VISITING MOM'S GRAVE? She texts.

Oh...yeah, I did. But I don't type that back or anything, and instead, put away my phone. I have other plans for tonight.

3

I T'S TIME TO meet ole Teddy Bear face-to-face. Teddy lives out in Loudoun County in a small house he inherited from his grandmother. It's an unfortunate house in that it looks like a kindly old lady threw up all over it. It's pink and green and complete with delicate latticework, a wraparound porch, white picket fence, rose bushes, and rocking chairs.

Hell, it's even got cherubs carved into the woodwork.

I've been here nearly every night, scoping things out, but tonight is the night I take it further.

I pull my Jeep up behind several other vehicles already here and climb out. I'm glad I'm one county over because if anyone who knew me saw how I'm currently dressed, they'd know something was up.

But I channel Daisy and all her friends for tonight. I've watched them enough to know the routine.

In my mini skirt, tank top, high heels, and makeup, I'm wearing the costume that'll get me in the door, that'll attract Teddy's attention. Flipping my hair over, I give it a quick tussle, and then I strut my ass over the stone walkway that leads up to the front door.

Music filters out, and through the windows, I see the same party I've seen nearly every night raging on. Without knocking, I turn the knob and stroll right on in.

A deep bass thumps the air that is heavy with the smell of pot. Laughter, voices, and the sounds of a video game hit me from all directions. If the outside looks like a grandmother threw up, the inside looks more like diarrhea complete with doilies, hand-sewn pillows, and antique furniture. I'm not sure why Teddy Bear kept this place looking like Granny, but whatever. To each their own, and all that.

Some high school dude spies me hanging by the door and sidles up. "Hey," he flirts, giving me what I'm sure he thinks is a sexy once over. "Haven't seen you here before."

I smile, flirting right back. "Keg?"

He thumbs over his left shoulder, and I slide past him, making sure our bodies brush, making sure I put a lot of sway in my hips as I stride away. Through the front parlor, I go, and I walk under an archway that leads into the living room.

And bingo. There's Teddy, all five foot five of him, soft rolls, and shaggy brown hair, relaxed back on a chaise lounge with a girl under each arm, looking like he's a damn sheik or something. I don't know how much money he inherited from Granny, but with all the cheap booze scattered about, it's probably going to last a while.

The girls look about my age and Teddy Bear's thirty-one. As evidenced by all the girls in the house, he definitely likes them young. He chuckles as the one on his right caresses his crotch, and then he spies me. New meat.

Slowly, I run my tongue along my top lip, drawing him in, then I turn, and trailing my fingers along the wall, I leave the living room and make my way into the kitchen. I'm leaning up against the counter, idly watching the boys around the keg when Teddy takes the bait and sidles in.

He doesn't waste a second moving right up to me, bracing his hands on both sides of the counter and bracketing me in. I slide my bored eyes off the keg and down into Teddy's soft face. In heels, I'm punching six feet, and this guy comes to my chest.

"What are you in the mood for?" he whispers, his breath rancid with cheap vodka.

I've got my eye makeup done all smoky, and I take a few seconds, really working them, staring at him, pulling him in. His hairy hand on the counter to the right of me slides off and onto my hip and then keeps right on going down past my mini skirt and onto my bare leg.

Flexing my thigh, I lean into his repulsive hand, and he gives me a happy shark smile. "Does the carpet match the drapes?"

What a douche. Did he really just ask me that?

His fingers scoot higher, wrapping around the back of my thigh. I'm tempted to see how far he'll go, but I need to stick to my plan. So I trail one manicured finger down the center of his soft chest and catch his belt loop.

I give a firm tug, and his erection bumps against me. I almost get impressed that he has one with all the alcohol streaming in his system. "Tomorrow night. Alone. Just you and me. Midnight." Then I lean down and graze his earlobe with my teeth before pushing past, leaving the house and his hard-on behind.

Once outside I spit his nasty ass ear taste out of my

mouth. Tomorrow night, Teddy, you and I are going to have a little meeting of the minds. Incompetence is rewarded more often than not, and he's about to win the gold medal in stupidity.

4

T A QUARTER till midnight on the following evening, I pull my Jeep into Teddy Bear's neighborhood, and I park a few blocks down. Dressed in cargo pants and a long sleeve black tee, I slip the bokken I use in Aikido class down inside its holder that is strapped to my back and beneath my tee.

Inside the right thigh cargo pocket, I place Pepper Spray, in the left a Taser, in the right calf cargo pocket goes my favorite nylon zip ties, and in the left calf pocket, I slip my lockpicks. I wrap my shoulder length curly hair in a quick ponytail and climb out.

Through the dark I jog, and as I step foot onto Teddy's property I lower the neoprene ski mask over my head. The place sits empty of cars, as I knew it would in Teddy's expectation of my arrival.

I hop over the white picket fence and head left through his unlit side yard. Up to the back porch I go, and before I even try picking the lock, I rotate the knob and find it open.

I slip into the mudroom, my ears tuned, but hear only silence. Beneath my mask, the stale smell of cigarettes and booze greets me, and I inch further in, now standing in the kitchen. Above the stove shines a yellow light and it illuminates the remnants of last night's party, or maybe one he had tonight. Teddy may have cleared the house of people in expectation of my arrival, but he didn't bother cleaning.

A muffled sound filters through my face mask, coming from the other side of the house. Maybe Teddy isn't alone after all. If he's expecting a threesome, he's pushing his luck. Plus a third person will put a huge kink in my plan.

Through the kitchen and across the living room I go and into the parlor where a door stands open on the other side. Shadows move, something crashes, and the muffled sounds transition into the distinct sound of fighting.

I take a deep breath and let it out slow and steady until I'm cold and focused. I coil tight, inching closer, coming up against the wall. I reach back for my bokken at the exact same second Teddy bursts from the bedroom, fumbling for footing, not even seeing me hovering along the wall. He races past, scrambling for the front door, and out he goes.

Right behind him surges someone else, another man, just a little bigger than Teddy. He catches sight of me in his peripheral vision and spins.

"Who are you?" he demands.

The whole thing happens so quickly, I'm not quite sure where things go wrong. He lunges, a knife out and ready. I block his lunge with my bokken, grab the knife, rotate my wrist, and the next thing I know the knife sinks right into his abdomen.

What the hell?

He makes a small gurgle of surprise before falling to a slump at my feet. It takes me a second of standing and staring down at his body to realize he's bleeding out.

Shit!

The knife must have severed his abdominal aorta. I take a step back and my brain scrambles. Do I help him? Do I run? I have no clue who this man is.

I take another step back. I have to help him. I'll find something for compression, dial 911, and get the hell out of here.

I whip around, looking for anything to use as compression. On the other side of the living room, I spy an open door that leads into a bathroom. I hurry across and in and grab all the towels I can find. I cross back over to the stabbed man, and my steps slow as I get closer.

He's not moving.

He's no longer gurgling.

He's dead.

I come here for Teddy and end up accidentally killing some random stranger. I have no clue who this guy is. If he's good, bad. For all I know he could have been here for the same reason I was, to rough Teddy up. To teach him a lesson.

I don't do things in the moment like this. I plan. I wait. Nothing's ever spontaneous.

I need to get out of here.

I throw the towels down, and my gaze catches on a phone laying on the floor. Teddy must have dropped it in his hasty escape. On a quick thought, I snatch it up and hurry back the way I came.

Back in my Jeep, I strip my gloves and mask, carefully inspecting my entire body for the unknown man's blood. I don't see any, but still, I strip, wadding my outfit up inside my duffle and slipping back into a pair of jeans and short sleeve tee.

I crank my engine and drive in a daze from the neighborhood and back onto the interstate. Four. I've now killed four people.

The serial killer, The Decapitator, was the first. Or rather my mother, though of course at the time I had no clue. She deserved it, there is no doubt in my mind of that, but afterward, I was off my game. For months I walked around in a haze, trying to make sense of everything I thought I knew.

Then Aunt Marji strolled into my life. My second kill, and again, I hold no reservation that she deserved it. She was just as disgusting as my mother. I told myself I was going to torture Marji only, but when I held that knife in my hands when she taunted me, rage surged through me and I couldn't stop the downward propulsion of the blade. Afterward, unlike with Mom's death, I didn't walk around in a haze. What happened with Marji empowered me.

Catalina, my copycat, was the third. Though in reality, she fell on her knife while we were fighting. I didn't plunge my blade into her body as I did with Aunt Marji. I could have helped Catalina, but I didn't. I didn't feel the boiling anger like I did with Marji, but I stood over Catalina and watched her die. She killed Dr. Issa and harmed so many others. Bleeding out was the least she deserved.

And now the fourth, this unknown and accidental man. Knives. After what happened with Mom and Aunt Marji, I wanted to leave that "inheritance" behind me. And here I am once again, death by a knife.

I try to grasp a thought or a feeling on the matter, but the numbness and haze in my brain remind me of the time span after The Decapitator. I need to make sense of the kill.

Forty-five minutes go by and I'm not entirely sure how or why, but I end up at Tommy's apartment and parking along the curb. He lives alone in a basement studio of someone's house. I spy his bike parked in the driveway and get a little irritated that he didn't tell me he was back.

Then again he may have just gotten home.

All that aside, the thought of seeing him has my heart picking up pace faster than it was forty-five minutes ago when I stabbed some random guy. It's beating fast like it was after Aunt Marji.

I find that curious.

Jumping from my Jeep, I stroll over, and the closer I get the more my skin buzzes. It takes him a few seconds to answer my knock and pure surprise flashes through his blue eyes. The last time I saw him, blonde stubble covered his cheeks that are now cleanly shaven. Bummer. I liked the stubble.

"Hey," he says. "How'd you know I was home? You stalking me?"

Sort of. I have driven by here a few times. "Don't flatter yourself," I say instead which makes him chuckle.

The sound of that chuckle, slow and methodical and coming from deep in his throat, has the buzzing along my skin crawling into my scalp. My fingers flex. I need something, but I'm not sure what.

Stepping back, he lets me in and my gaze tracks over to the black saddle bag sitting beside the door and the black leather jacket draped over top. I guess he really did just get in.

He slides behind me, closing the door, and his scent, a mixture of leather and soap, wafts through my senses and turns me on quicker than anything Dr. Issa ever did. I turn to face Tommy and find him leaning up against the door, his arms folded, staring at me.

My body temp ratchets up several degrees, and I have the unnerving desire to strip naked.

I rotate my neck, and my gaze eats up his blonde hair that's grown out since the last time I saw him, thick and a bit of wave to it. My eyes track down across the curve of his tattooed bicep, over the firm line of his pecs, further down his flat abs, and all the way to trail his long-muscled legs.

My nerve endings stretch. I don't know what's going on with my body. Maybe it's the kill and delayed aftershocks, or maybe it's Tommy. Hell, it's probably a combination of both, but my gaze comes back up to meet his, and in the time I was visually devouring his body, something shifted in his eyes. An awareness, sure, but a heat, too. A hunger.

He's feeling this, too.

"You cut your hair," he says, his voice low, and I don't respond. I don't even nod, as my mind dives into dark and carnal images of our bodies pressed together. They flick through my head in rapid fire, but it's the last one my brain latches onto. Me on my knees, undoing his belt.

"Everything okay?" he whispers.

Again, I don't respond. Instead, I do exactly what I want. I drop to my knees and undo his pants.

Afterward, Tommy's still standing propped against the door, and I get to my feet. I watch as he slowly puts his jeans back together and then he pushes off the door and steps forward. His eyes touch the features of my face. "You do realize we've never even kissed."

"You complaining?"

"Uh, that would be a no." His strong fingers slide through my hair and he brings his lips to mine. The kiss goes long and firm and when he pulls back, he nips my bottom lip. "I'm in the mood for Jell-O."

My lips twitch. "Jell-O?"

He nods. "Jell-O."

I follow him into the kitchen where he retrieves two Jell-

O cups from the refrigerator. One cherry and one lime. I take the lime and in silence, we stare at each other as we eat our treat. I don't want my mind to, but it wanders to the unknown man I stabbed. I need to find out who it is.

"Where'd you just go?" Tommy asks, tossing his empty cup into the garbage.

I forgot how good he is at reading me. "Nowhere," I say, tossing mine away, too.

"What made you come here?" He asks next.

I don't answer because I'm not sure. I accidentally kill someone and my body on autopilot brings me here. My mother butchered Tommy's sister, though of course he doesn't know this, and our relationship has been one giant roller coaster since then. But somewhere along the way, Tommy must have become my safe place.

"Got another Jell-O?" I ask instead of answering his question because oddly enough lime Jell-O just officially became my new favorite thing.

His lips twitch, mirroring mine. "All out."

I sigh. "Well, whatever will you do for dessert now?"

Tommy chuckles and the sound of it vibrates through my stomach. I turn away before I get down on my knees again and cross back over to his door.

"Next time I'll return the favor," he speaks as I open the door.

I don't turn around, but I do smile. Hell, yeah, he's going to return the favor.

THE NEXT MORNING I open my laptop and do a quick search of Loudoun County news, trying to figure out who I killed. Right there it is front and center, and holy freaking shit.

I killed Scott Butler, son of the District Attorney, which means this thing's about to become huge. District Attorney Butler is well-liked and known for going after and putting away the bad guys. She's got a hard-ass reputation. If she had been handling Teddy's case, I guarantee you he wouldn't have gotten off on some evidence technicality.

Though I've never met her, she and Victor go way back, like high school back. I'm not certain, but it seems like I remember him mentioning they went to Homecoming together. Watch her turn out to be the one that "got away". Wouldn't that just be my luck?

I do a quick search of Scott Butler and read that he was a well-loved Guidance Counselor at a local high school. The article speculates that he was at Teddy's house, confronting him about the girl who was killed. Apparently, the girl was a student where Scott worked.

So he did go to Teddy's house for the same reason I was there—to confront Teddy—and it ended with me accidentally stabbing him.

Talk about being in the wrong place at the wrong time.

LATER THAT DAY after my Patch and Paw shift, I find myself back in Loudoun County and parked down the street from Teddy's house. The police have barricaded the area and numerous neighbors stand clumped on this side of the barricade watching the cops move in and out of Teddy's house.

Slipping on my shades, I merge with the neighbors, watching, listening... I need to know what the police really think. More importantly, do they suspect a third party was in the house?

"Brutal struggle..."

"...Stab wound to the abdomen."

"Some dipshit rookie walked through the scene..."

"...Ted Lowman's gonna wish he was dead."

"He's the guy who killed that high school girl and got away..."

"...shit ton of drugs in the house."

"Wonder where Ted ran to..."

"...this is about as high profile as it gets."

I listen carefully, taking it all in. I'm not sure how the

neighbors know all of this, but I assume many of them have been out here for hours. I should be happy people think Ted Lowman is guilty of the stabbing, but I'm not. Maybe if I had accidentally stabbed someone who deserved it, I would be. As it is, though, Scott Butler is the hero in this story and more alive in my thoughts than dead.

"I knew this house was trouble..."

"...maybe Ted's hiding out somewhere local."

I doubt it. Ted Lowman is long gone. He's not coming back. Not with people thinking he killed the D.A.'s son.

Beside me, someone sighs, heavy and deep, and moving only my eyes I glance to the left and to the boy standing there. He's the only one in this clump of neighbors who hasn't said a word.

Behind my sunglasses, I size him up. He's about my height and looks a bit younger, like Daisy's age, sixteen or so. With his dark curly hair, black-rimmed glasses, pale skin, and slender build, I imagine he spends his days playing video games more than anything else.

Under his breath, he snorts and shakes his head. "Look at her, all high and mighty."

My gaze tracks back over to Teddy's house and the cops going in and out. On the porch stands District Attorney Butler, her dark hair chic short and her blue pantsuit perfectly pressed. She's focused intently on whatever the detective is saying.

My eyes trail over her petite body and perfect posture, and the first thing I think of is my stepdad. He knew her in high school. He went with her to Homecoming. I find this interesting. I've only ever known him with my mom, but of course, he had a life before her.

"'I've dedicated my life to fighting crime'," the boy

beside me mumbles. "'To keeping our streets safe'." With a scoff, the boy turns away. "Good luck with this one, *Mom*."

Whoa, hold up. Did he just say "Mom"? As in the D.A.? Well, this is interesting. "Excuse me," I say, turning away from the neighborhood clump and trailing behind the boy. "Did I just hear you right? Is the D.A. your mom?"

The boy doesn't even look at me as he keeps walking. "That's right."

"So you're the victim's younger brother?"

"Yeah, and his name was Scott, not victim, and if you say 'sorry for your loss' I'm going postal."

I don't say anything, but I do keep following him. He's definitely piqued my interest.

The boy turns then, pushing his glasses up, and now that I'm really looking at his face, I definitely see the resemblance from the picture I saw of Scott on the news. Dark curly hair, pale skin, freckles, light brown eyes.

The fact is his brother, Scott, was here and had a knife on him. He was trying to harm Teddy, or at least he was thinking of harming Teddy. Then when Scott saw me, he got startled and attacked. Maybe he was here on a purely noble mission to avenge a student's death, but something's not sitting right.

Yes, my gut tells me something else is going on.

"They say Scott fought like a hero, but that he was overmatched. Fatal stab, bled out instantly. Didn't suffer." The boy thumbs himself in the chest. "I want to know why. I want to understand what happened. I thought coming here and looking would help me make sense of his death. But...I can't believe he's gone." Behind his glasses, he rubs his light brown eyes, then blinks at me. "You ever lost anybody?"

Through my shades, I look at this boy whose name I don't even know. I'm not sure what to make of him. He seemed cynical at first and now full of a depth I wasn't expecting. "Yes," I find myself telling him. "My mom."

"That sucks."

To that, I don't respond.

"People really loved him, ya know? He even got teacher of the year."

No, I don't know, but I nod.

"I mean he wasn't perfect, but..." With a sigh, the boy looks away. "Well, I guess I'm going to go."

With a nod, I watch him walk over to an old Chevy and climb inside, then he cranks the engine and drives away. That was the oddest conversation I think I've ever had.

The neighborhood looky-loos begin to break apart and wander off. Two stroll right past me. "Whatever," the woman on the right says. "I've seen that Scott guy here before. He's no hero Guidance Counselor defending the honor of the dead girl. He and Ted Lowman had something else going on."

And there it is. I turn to head back to my Jeep and catch sight of District Attorney Butler still standing on the porch, but she's no longer talking to the detective, she's staring across the yard and the police barricade right at me.

THAT EVENING I walk inside my home and see my family in the living room watching a movie. I note that it's Dirty Dancing, Mom's favorite.

My stepdad pauses the movie, glancing over at me. "Missed you at the grave," he says, getting right to the point, and his tone is like a slap to the face.

It's been a couple of days. I'm surprised he's choosing now to bring it up. Maybe because they're watching Mom's movie.

My gaze tracks over to Daisy to see her looking back at me with the exact expression Victor has—disappointment, hurt, and a touch of anger. I glance to Justin next to see his dark head bowed over a comic book, reading. I think Daisy and Victor could use a lesson from Justin in moving on.

Daisy's blue eyes narrow. "I texted you to remind you."

"I know."

With a sigh, Daisy looks at Victor, I guess expecting him to reprimand me or something. It's interesting to me how close Daisy is to Mom now that she's dead.

"So," Daisy says, pushing at me verbally, "you're just going to stop visiting Mom's grave?"

I look between my stepdad and Daisy. "I'm in a different place than you two. I don't want to visit Mom's grave, and you need to respect that. Just like I respect the fact that you *want* to visit her."

A couple of seconds go by while everyone apparently thinks about what I just said, then with a nod, Victor gets up from the couch and crosses the living room to where I still stand at the front door. He wraps me up in a warm and secure hug, and a very distinct sensation of love moves through me.

"You're right," he tells me. "You grieve how you want to."

He pulls away, and I look up into his eyes. That sensation of love transitions into something even deeper, and I truly mean it when I say, "I love you, Dad." I forget how much he likes it when I call him that.

"I love you, too, sweetie."

My eyes cut over to Daisy and Justin. "I love both of you very much."

Daisy's hostility merges with a flash of tenderness, and she gets this confused expression like she's not quite sure how the air in the room shifted. "Did you just say you *loved* us?"

Of course, I've said it before, but not as often as I probably should. "Yes, I did."

Justin finally glances up from his comic book. "Of course Lane loves us. Leave her alone."

With a chuckle, Victor moves into the kitchen. "M&Ms with our popcorn?"

"Yeah!" Justin yells, jumping up.

Victor cuts me a quick glance. "If I pick another movie, will you join us?"

"Yes," I don't hesitate in saying. "Let me just run upstairs and I'll be right back."

I take the steps two at a time, smiling, actually looking forward to going back down and hanging out with my family.

The only thing I want to do is run a quick search on Scott Butler and specifically his little brother's name. But when I open my laptop, the headline on my news feed catches my attention and the attached girl's photo.

It's the same girl who was snuggling on the couch with old Teddy Bear, or more importantly, caressing his crotch. The headline reads:

GIRL FOUND STRANGLED

STRANGLED. It's the same way he allegedly killed the other girl. Looks like Teddy's in the area after all.

THE NEXT MORNING Daisy and I stand in the kitchen staring out into the living room where Justin and his friends are hanging out. Somehow we got wrangled into watching them this morning. I like kids. They're fun to play with, or rather I enjoy watching them play, but I know with one hundred percent certainty that I don't want any of my own.

I would never take the chance of passing down my warped genetics. Plus, what kind of mom would I be? I've killed people.

"You know, sometimes I look at kids and wonder what they'll grow up to be." Daisy nods to one digging at his armpit. "Dermatologist."

She points to one who just sneezed chocolate milk. "Science teacher."

She nods to another who is re-tying his shoe. "Garbage collector."

I cut her an amused look. "Why is that one a garbage collector?"

Daisy shrugs. "No reason. Someone needed to be."

I study each one of them, and my eyes fall on the quietest one in the group. Watching, listening, but not really participating, and I wonder if he's really part of the group or if his parents made him come. That one, the quiet one, would have been me. I should note that kid's name and a couple of years from now check up on him. I'd be curious to see who he becomes.

Children are our future, but right now staring at these boys, I don't really see it. Well, except for that quiet one. I could see him being any number of things, I think. "What about the quiet one?" I ask Daisy.

"Serial killer, for sure."

I'M FEELING OFF, and I know it has everything to do with killing Scott Butler. Ted Lowman may have originally gotten off on some mishandling-of-evidence technicality, but with the D.A. now personally involved, every "t" will be crossed and every "i" dotted. Count on it.

I have to get to Teddy before the D.A. and her crew does. I was at that party, and the recently strangled girl was there, too, sitting right by Teddy. It won't be long before the cops link her to him, and everyone else who was there, including me. Which is why I need to find and take care of Teddy. Because as soon as he's officially off the radar, the D.A. will have her justice and will move on.

This burner phone Teddy dropped has to cough up something. It has to.

Someone knocks on my bedroom door, and I recognize the soft rap of knuckles as Victor. When Daisy knocks it's all bony and staccato. When Justin knocks it's a smack of the palm. Mom used to knock with her nails.

I stash Teddy's burner phone under my mattress. "Come in."

Victor cracks open the door and peeks around the corner. "You've heard of District Attorney Butler, right?"

I blink. "Of course. Didn't you date her in high school?"

Now it's Victor's turn to blink. "You remember that?"

"Yes."

He chuckles. "It was only a few dates. Anyway, she recently lost one of her boys."

"I know. I heard. It was in the news."

"Yes, of course. Anyway, I'm going over to her house later. Was wondering if you could watch Justin?"

Hm, District Attorney Butler's home. Now that's a place I wouldn't mind seeing. Maybe snooping around a bit. See if I can get to know the person I killed a little better. See if I can talk to the little brother again. He did intrigue me.

"Actually, you mind if I go with you? I met the younger brother and wouldn't mind seeing how he's doing."

"You met Adam?" Victor blinks again, this time surprised.

Adam. So that's the younger brother's name. "I did."

"Oh, okay. I'll get Daisy to watch Justin." He checks his watch. "How about in an hour?"

And just like that, I'm about to step foot in the Butler home.

V ICTOR PULLS THROUGH the open white gate and up the driveway to park in a circular entrance. District Attorney Butler lives in a McMansion in Great Falls, and as I get out of Victor's car, my gaze roams over the sprawling stone and brick multi-level home. This place has to be upwards of seven thousand square feet, not to mention the nearly three acres of manicured land it sits on.

From the backseat, he grabs the lasagna he made and together we climb the three wide steps up to the porch. I've never understood why people feel the need to bring food when someone dies. After Mom died, our kitchen was inundated with casseroles and cookies. I'm fairly confident I can go the rest of my life without ever seeing another covered dish.

At least Victor made lasagna and not some chicken cream thing that seemed to be the theme of what everyone brought us.

He presses the doorbell and even it sounds rich as it gongs slowly and melodically. A few seconds later, the deep burgundy door swings open and there stands District Attorney Butler dressed casually in jeans, a polo, and platform sandals. And where before she wore her chic short hair smoothed back, now she wears it more tousled and funky.

She doesn't even glance at me as she smiles gently and welcomes Victor with a familiar hug. It makes me wonder when exactly they saw each other last. It can't be high school because that hug seemed too easy and warm.

Pulling back, Victor turns to me. "This is my daughter, Lane."

Ms. Butler recognizes me immediately from the crime scene and surprise flicks across her eyes when she does.

So I decide to take the lead, holding out my hand. "It's very nice to meet you. I talked briefly with your younger son and didn't get a chance to formally introduce myself." There, that way she doesn't think I'm hiding something.

I redirect the conversation. "You have a beautiful home."

"Thank you." With that, Ms. Butler steps aside and lets us in.

Where usually people have their houses too warm, the Butlers keep theirs crisp and cold, and I fall immediately in love. My core temperature runs hot and more than half the time I'm uncomfortably warm.

The entry spans over oak floors into a bright and open first story. Taking the lasagna from Victor, Ms. Butler leads the way down a wide hall in the direction of—I'm assuming—the kitchen. As she does, I trail behind, my gaze popping in and out of the rooms. A living room over to the right. A formal dining room to the left. A den right beside it.

A den where Adam just happens to be. I catch sight of his curly head slouched down on a couch, earbuds in, as he stares at whatever's on his laptop screen. He doesn't glance up, and I doubt he even knows we're here.

Ms. Butler treads into the kitchen, placing the lasagna on the marble island next to a row of covered dishes others have brought by. She takes a second, closing her eyes, breathing, clearly trying to get herself in control, and I take that as my cue to leave.

"Dad," I whisper. "I saw Adam in the other room. I'm going to go say hi."

Victor nods, and as I leave, I see him stepping forward, his hand out, ready to console her. I don't know if there is a Mr. Butler, and frankly, I don't care. If Victor and the D.A. want to bond over this, more power to them.

Backtracking my steps, I make my way into the den done with soft yellow leather couches and a flat screen T.V. that takes up the whole wall. Adam doesn't notice my entrance so captivated by whatever is on his laptop, and so I use the available moment to snoop.

I wander over to a floor-to-ceiling bookcase and note an entire collection of Encyclopedias. Who the hell has actual Encyclopedias these days? But what my eyes fixate on are the myriad of framed photos.

Hm. I move in for a better look.

There are dozens of them mixed and matched, old and new, casual and formal. There's one of a man I assume must be the father. Unlike my family and all our mixtures of hair and eye color, this family—with their dark hair and pale skin—definitely looks related.

"That's my father," comes a voice from behind me. "He was a drunk and pretty much an entire waste of a life."

I catch the "was" in that sentence and don't ask. Instead, I turn and look into the familiar face of the boy from yesterday. He's still sitting on the couch, looking over his shoulder at me.

"I'm Lane. I hear your name is Adam. Our parents know each other."

He cocks his head. "Is that why you were there yesterday?"

"Yes." That and the fact I accidentally killed your brother.

Pulling his earbuds out, Adam lays the laptop aside and pushes up from the couch. His gaze drifts back over to the father's picture. "A drunk and an abusive bastard. Scott got the worst of it. Took the hits for me, too."

I'm surprised he's so share-y with the details. "Sounds like your brother was a stand-up guy."

Adam nods. "He was. Last conversation I had with him was about Dad."

"Oh?"

"My brother worried way too much about the whole nature versus nurture thing. He wondered all the time how much of Dad was in him." Adam lets out a half-hearted chuckle. "I suppose he's in me, too, right?"

I don't know what to say because this hits way too close to home, and again I'm surprised Adam is sharing so much information. "Yes, he's in both of you, but you are your own person and you decide what to do with that."

Adam moves across the oak floor, coming to stand beside me. "I like that."

Now that I know the dad is a mean one, I turn from Adam to study the dad's face. In one of the family photos, they're standing on a ledge overlooking the Grand Canyon. Adam looks young, maybe five, and Scott around fifteen or so. Though they're all standing close, none of them are touching, and all of them have barely-there smiles like they know they're supposed to smile but they don't want to.

"Mom keeps reassuring me they'll find the guy who did it." Adam picks up a photo of him and Scott on four-wheelers, and with a sigh, studies it. "I hate when she reassures me."

"Why is that?"

"Because I feel like she's just trying to make me feel better versus telling me the truth. I'd rather she be straight with me."

This boy has quite the insight. "How old are you?" I ask.

"Sixteen."

"You think your mom's going to find Ted Lowman?"

Adam scoffs. "If anything to get her shot in court."

He does a lot of scoffing when it comes to his mom.

Adam puts the framed photo back on the shelf. "I'd rather see him die a violent death."

O-kay. Interesting. "And how are you going to accomplish that?"

Folding his arms, he props his shoulder on the bookshelf and looks at me. "I have my ways of doing just about anything."

I mirror his posture, propping my shoulder, too, facing him. "I take it your mom doesn't know about these 'ways'."

He shrugs. "My mom doesn't know anything about me."

Yeah, this boy has definitely piqued my interest, and I'm wondering if Adam's "ways" may lead him to Teddy before I can get to him. As soon I get out of here, I'm going to check that burner phone again.

Adam pushes off the bookcase and treads back over to the couch. He grabs his laptop and slides it back onto his lap. "You said you lost your mom. How long until it doesn't hurt?"

"Mom will always be in my memory," I truthfully say, though the world is better off without her. The question is— is the world better off without Scott?

Adam obviously loves his older brother, and I am the reason why Adam is now an only child. Whichever way this goes, I owe this boy something, yet I'm not quite sure what.

"Ready?" Victor asks, peeking his head in the open door.

"Yes," I say because I need to find Teddy. ASAP.

"**B**ABY, YOU OKAY?** I heard something horrible happened at your Granny's house. If you need a place to stay, don't forget about Uncle Chuck's cabin out at River Hall. It's number eight and there's always a spare key under that ceramic frog thingy of his. I'm going to call your other number, too. Mommy loves you!"

This is the message Ted Lowman's "mommy" leaves on the disposable phone he dropped in his haste to evacuate Granny's house.

It's been one day since I spoke with Adam. One day of incessantly checking the burner phone. Before I would have just called my whiz of a friend, Reggie, to find some leads on Teddy, but after our fall out, I still don't know where Reggie and I stand. So this burner phone is it for me, and just when I thought it would be a dead end, that voicemail came in and my luck officially changed.

So here I am in my Jeep, smiling, and if I did listen to music, right now *Lollipop* would be a great song to match my cheery mood. Nothing like a good lead and an even better hunt to lift my spirits. Except I promised Victor I would be back in a couple of hours. As soon as I start college and move out, I won't have to deal with this lack of freedom anymore. I'll have the luxury of staying out all night if I want.

For now, though, my living arrangements are full of pros and cons. The biggest pro being Justin's smile, and the biggest con—making promises I don't necessarily want to keep. Yes, things won't be so complicated once I'm on my own.

Or so I tell myself.

For now, though, I'll check out Uncle Chuck's cabin and see what there is to see. I have to hope Adam and/or the case detectives haven't been effective in following leads. With the burner phone and Mommy's message, I have to hope I'm ahead of them on this.

If things would've gone as planned, Scott might still be alive, I wouldn't be on the Butler's radar, Adam would be playing his video games and none the wiser, and I wouldn't be chasing a clock trying to beat the D.A. and her team in finding Teddy.

If things would have gone as planned...

I only have a couple of hours to check out Uncle Chuck's place. And checking out is all I intend to do. If he's there I'll come back later after everyone is asleep.

...don't forget about Uncle Chuck's cabin out at River Hall. It's number eight.

A quick search of River Hall delivered me back one hit— a hunting camp in Loudoun County. According to the Internet, it's nestled within the woods with thirty secluded cabins that provide individual privacy and escape from the rigors of the city.

Perfect.

I pull off the county road, following the signs for River

Hall and wind my way down a gravel road. My headlights cut through the early evening darkness, and I nearly miss the wood sign with white painted RIVER HALL lettering. I cut my lights to dim and pull through the open chain link gate.

One lone yellow light illuminates a building off to the left and I read OFFICE painted on the wood door. The gravel road forks, one narrow lane going right and the other left, merging all the way in the back. From my internet search, I know number eight is located to the right. But I go left. I want to see the lay of the land.

Cutting my lights all the way, I navigate by the yellow lamps attached intermittently to the trees. Thick vegetation swallows each cabin and my tires softly crunch over the gravel as I inch my way along.

I pass number thirty, twenty-nine, twenty-eight, and the cabins keep going down in number, all empty. When I make it to nineteen, I spy a dirt bike sitting in front of the log cabin and one lone pale white light coming from inside. I can't see who is there but with the dirt bike, I'm assuming only one person.

I keep going—cabin number eighteen, seventeen, and sixteen sit empty, too.

I don't know a whole lot about hunting but I'm guessing maybe summer isn't really a good time for the sport. Or perhaps the place is empty because it's a weekday.

Eight comes into view and like all the others, it sits dark inside. I keep driving, crawling along the gravel, my tires chomping quietly beneath me. Cabin six, five, four... all empty.

I finish the circular tour, coming to a stop back at the office. Checking my phone, I see I still have time to spare, so with my lights still out, I turn my Jeep around and backtrack to number five, parking in its vacant and dark spot, tucking my Jeep as far into the trees as possible.

Uncle Chuck's cabin is three over from me, and Teddy's not in there. Other than the one cabin at the other side of the hunting camp, the entire area sits empty.

I don't bother donning my disguise or grabbing my gear. I do slip gloves on though, in case I decide to prowl around inside, and I grab my lockpicks. Climbing from my Jeep, I quietly click the door closed and take off in a light jog through the trees.

A few seconds later I come upon number eight and crouch in the shadows to give it a good study. Heavy curtains cover the windows, making everything dark. Built of dark wood slats with a tiny screened in front porch, the place can't be more than five or six hundred square feet.

Yes, from the outside it looks like it's been empty for a while, but once I'm inside I'll be able to tell if Teddy's been here.

I emerge from my cover and slip down the side around to the back, and as I'd hoped, there's a back door. Three wood steps lead up to it, and I first try the handle, not surprised to find it locked. With my picks, it doesn't take but a few seconds to pop it open.

The door opens into a kitchen, and my eyes fall on one single dirty bowl in the sink. Someone has definitely been here.

I move quietly across the worn linoleum, my senses tuned. A wood panel, foldable door separates the kitchen from what I assume must be the living room. The panel sits open several inches, wide enough for a slender person to slip through sideways.

Beyond the gap in the door, a dim light flickers, like a nightlight holding on to its last bit of juice.

Turning sideways, I slink through the door and out the other side, coming to an immediate stop. Teddy is most definitely here, lying sprawled on his back, his wide unseeing eyes staring at the ceiling and a butcher knife sticking out of his chest.

But what really halts my movement is the person kneeling beside him—Adam Butler. With blood smeared on his gloved hands and glasses slid to the end of his nose, he's very quiet and still as he stares down at the knife. I don't want to jump to conclusions here. Adam may not have done this. He may have found Teddy like this.

The question is, did Adam follow Teddy here? He must have.

I study the blood beneath Teddy's body, no longer creeping out and more thick and coagulated on the striped area rug stretched beneath him. I'm no expert in blood patterns, but I would estimate Teddy's been that way a while, which would explain Adam's calm demeanor. He's had a chance to ride the nerves and is now coming down off the high.

Adam senses my presence and his head jerks up. His eyes widen. "Wh-what are you doing here?" He goes to move, rolling to his feet, and I hold my hands up. "It's okay. You're okay."

Adam takes a few seconds, weighing my words and the situation. "I-I didn't mean to. Or maybe I did. I don't know. I really just wanted to see who he was and the next thing I knew I had a knife in my hand, and I stabbed him."

Adam takes a step away, and still with my hands up I carefully say, "Adam, it's okay. I'm not going to tell anyone. Okay? But you can't move. You can't track evidence around the cabin."

With a deep breath, Adam nods, looking back down at

Teddy. "He killed my brother and got away with it. That's not fair." Adam glances up at me. "You know?"

"I do know." Slowly, I lower my hands and just as slowly I slide the rest of the way into the living room. "I'm going to help you, okay? I promise."

"He choked the life out of that girl. He stabbed my brother."

No, I stabbed your brother, and I officially owe you for that.

"Should we call my mom?"

I shake my head. "No, Adam, you can't do that."

"B-but it was self-defense."

"Was it?"

Adam doesn't immediately answer, and I know in my gut that it most certainly was not self-defense. "I can help, Adam, if you let me."

"I'm pretty good at worming around cyberspace. I stumbled across this cabin that belonged to an Uncle. It was a long shot coming here. I didn't think..."

He mentioned having his "ways" and he certainly delivered. But if Adam stumbled across this property, it won't be long before the D.A. and her team does, too.

"I was just going to see, you know? Then I was going to tell Mom. She'd be so proud of me for finding Scott's killer. You know? I didn't expect he'd really be here. I mean, I hoped, but... He surprised me. He jumped me. I didn't know what to do. I fought back. The knife ended up in him. I wasn't sure I could do it."

Adam's rambling, justifying, talking himself in and out of this. Whether he's ready to admit it or not, he came here with intent, and he obviously has mom issues. Don't we all? "I know," I keep assuring him. "It's okay. But we can't call your mom. She would *not* be happy with this or you."

That seemingly gets his attention, and he finally looks away from Teddy and up to me. He makes an awful face like disgust and confusion are competing for space. "What are we going to do?"

I like that he used "we", and though he hasn't asked me the specifics of how I came to be here, he will eventually, and I'll have to come up with a plausible story. But for now, I tell him, "I'm going to help you get rid of the evidence."

12

TOGETHER WE ROLL Teddy up in the striped rug, leaving the knife right where it is. "How did you get here?" I ask Adam.

"My car. I parked it behind one of the cabins." He casts a nervous glance around the dark living room. "I was careful."

Still, with the calm voice, I continue, "Okay, take your bloody gloves off and put them inside the rug. Grab a towel from the kitchen and use that on the doorknob. Careful of fingerprints. Go get your car and come back. Leave your headlights off." I glance around the room. "We need plastic."

"I brought a roll," he hurries to say.

Yes, this boy came here with intent. "Good. Bring the roll in."

"Okay. Okay." Quickly he strips his gloves, tosses them on top of a rolled-up Teddy, and disappears out the back door. While he's gone I look under Teddy and see a dark smudge where the blood seeped into the wood floor.

Careful not to touch anything, I look around the small cabin and find only one old bottle of Pine Sol. We'll clean it the best we can with that, take the rug from the small bedroom, and lay it over the spot. A coffee table on top and that's the best we've got.

Outside, Adam's tires crunch over the gravel as he pulls in. A few seconds later he comes back through the door, a roll of black plastic under his arm and a fresh pair of gloves on. Together we work at folding Teddy and his rug in the plastic and carrying him out to Adam's trunk.

Then we go about cleaning the floor, moving the rug from the bedroom, and putting the small coffee table on top.

Standing, we survey the area. My gaze carefully touches on every inch. From the couch to the rug. From one corner to the next. Up and down the walls. I even study the ceiling. I think briefly about just burning the place down.

"What do you think?" Adam asks.

"Well, seeing as how I've never cleaned a place of evidence, I honestly don't know."

"I read somewhere that if you take a blower to a crime scene, it'll scatter the evidence and confuse things."

I shift to look at him. "Let me guess, you've got a blower, too?"

He gives a sheepish shrug. "In my car."

"Well, go get it."

He's back within seconds, we plug the blower in and proceed to scatter dust and particles and whatever else through the cabin. Then we're out the door, I climb in my Jeep, Adam in his old Chevy, and we pull away from Uncle Chuck's cabin.

Adam follows me all the way to Patch and Paw, closed now for the evening. I punch my personal code into the keypad on the back door. I do a quick sweep of the facility, making sure it is indeed empty, and then we haul Teddy to the cremation room and slide him in.

The flames ignite, incinerating all the evidence. Last

year I stood in this exact spot doing a visual estimation of the opening, realizing it was big enough for a body. Now I know for sure it is.

Silently we leave. He gets in his car. I get in mine. And without looking at each other, we drive off in different directions. Whether I wanted to be or not, Adam and I are now inexorably linked.

13

THE NEXT MORNING I'm the first in the door at Patch and Paw, and I go straight to the cremation room and dispose of the ashes and bone fragments. I do keep a small amount back, just in case. One never knows when evidence might be needed. Then I check the list of borders, and I smile when I see Corn Chip's name.

For as long as I've worked here, Corn Chip has been coming. The first time I met him, he walked right up to me, lifted his leg, and peed on my shoe.

At that moment I knew we would get along famously, and indeed we do.

It's been weeks since his mom boarded him, and I've missed the little guy. I open the door to the room that houses the midsized kennels and am greeted with exuberant yapping.

I press the button that releases their hatches and they all scramble into the hall and straight down to the door that leads to the outside play area. Except for Corn Chip, he bee-lines it directly to me.

Leaning down, I give his gray scraggly head a good rub and a kiss. "Missed you, Little Guy."

But I know him, and I know he'll lose his bladder if I don't get him outside.

I'm not in my own little slice of heaven for more than five minutes when the new doctor steps into my peaceful domain. "Good morning, Lane!"

As a response, I nod. I swear to God if she asks me to express an anal gland today, I'm going to make sure it squirts right in her face.

Smiling at the yapping and playing dogs, Dr. O'Neal inhales a deep breath and lets out a loud and dramatic *aaah*. "Feel those lungs opening up. Try it, Lane."

I cut her a look.

She grins. "Try it."

One of my eyelids twitches. This is absolutely the most annoying person in my life.

Her grin gets even bigger if that's possible. "Try it."

I give a sharp inhale, then blow it right back out. There I tried it.

"See?" Dr. O'Neal laughs, going into a lunge and lifting her hands to the sky in what I'm sure is some sort of warrior pose. "Now really open up and take in the earth's energy."

I could probably Taser, zip tie, and toss her in a corner before she realized what happened. Maybe then she and her warrior energy will leave me alone.

Another deep breath in. "Be one with the sunlight. Send all your negative vibes into the ground."

I'll keep my negative vibes, thank you very much.

Another *aaah* from the annoying Dr. Issa replacement, then she comes out of her warrior pose to move uncomfortably close to me. So close I can smell the shampoo on her hair. "I noticed you alphabetized the borders' names. Good thinking."

I take a step away. I don't need to smell her shampoo. "Yes," I simply reply. I alphabetize everything. It only makes sense.

"I made a fresh batch of coffee. How do you take yours, sugar?"

"No."

"Cream?"

"No."

Another grin. "You're not much of a conversationalist, are you?"

No, and Dr. Issa got that about me. For that matter, so does everyone else around here. Pointless conversation is an art I do not excel in.

Through the side gate, I see a familiar car pull in. Crap, what is Adam doing here? "Excuse me," I say to Dr. O'Neal and make my way back through the clinic and outside.

"What are you doing here?" I ask, not even bothering to make niceties.

Adam casts a nervous glance around the parking lot that has only my Jeep and Dr. O'Neal's SUV. Then he brings his light brown eyes to mine. "What were you doing there at the cabin last night?"

Ah, I knew it would circle around to this, and I'm ready with my response. "I lost my mom to a violent death. You lost your brother. I felt like that somehow made us connected, and I wanted to help find Teddy. I wanted to help right a wrong. You're not the only one skilled with the ability to worm around the Internet."

Some truth, some lie, but it all must appease him because he closes his bloodshot eyes and nods. I'd lay a bet he didn't sleep the whole night. "How you holding up?" I ask.

He gives a weary nod. "I miss Scott."

"It gets easier."

"Does it really?"

"Yes, at least for me it is."

His eyes open back up. "We need to figure out a way to get my mom to stop the investigation. If there's one thing I can say about her, she's good at her job, and she won't give up until Ted Lowman is found."

"What are you talking about?"

"I mean, maybe if we would have planted the body somewhere, then she would have found it, and then she could have closed the case." He glances across the parking lot at Patch and Paw.

"It's too late," I assure him. "The ashes are gone. You need to let things die down on their own."

He scrubs his fingers through his messy dark hair. "She'll never let this die down. She'll go to her grave trying to find Scott's killer."

Okay, yeah, I can see where this might be a problem.

"I heard her on the phone this morning. They found another strangled girl. They think Teddy did it. Time of death just a few hours ago." Adam leans back against his car, crossing one ankle over the other. "You and I both know that can't be."

Yes, which also now means the other two may not be Teddy's either, which would mean he's innocent. Yet somehow I don't buy it. Something was definitely up with Teddy.

Stranglers typically stay with a type, and the first two had been young with dark hair. I'll have to see what the third one looks like.

"Also, I heard Mom say something about a scarf."

"I'm sorry, what?"

Adam nods. "Whoever strangled her did it with a scarf."

Huh, the first two girls had been strangled with hands. Or at least I think...

"Then I heard her say something about being linked, and that was also the moment she realized I was listening and walked off, so I couldn't hear anymore."

Linked. As in connected to another case. Or rather cases. I need to find out if the first two strangled girls were done with a scarf as well. But if there's one thing I've learned from snooping through Mom's FBI files, the authorities always keep something back. They keep a detail to themselves. This scarf thing might be that detail.

Adam gives his car keys a twirl and cocking his head, he studies me. "You seem fine with all of this."

Oh, you have no idea. I come from one twisted family. A little disposing of a body and talk of strangulation really is nothing. But that's not what he's looking for. He's looking for a sign I'm normal, so I take in a breath and blow it out, then rub my eyes. "To be honest, I didn't sleep so well. I guess I'm just in a major fog."

With a nod, Adam pushes off his car. "Well, thanks for being a friend."

Is that what we are? Yes, I guess so.

A car pulls into the parking lot, a burgundy Kia, and we both give it a glance. It's the receptionist, which means the rest of the staff will be arriving soon. She gives us both a cursory glance as she parks and climbs out before heading inside.

"My dad drove a car like that," Adam murmurs. "Son of a drunk bitch used to pile me and Scott in the back to go on liquor runs or to bars. We used to sit in the back with the windows open and listen to him brag about his accomplishments, and the more he drank, the bigger of a man he became." Adam huffs an unamused laugh. "Ran right off the road one night and straight into the Potomac. Scott's the one who pulled me from the car and swam me to safety."

I want to ask where their mom was during all of this, but I don't.

"Scott used to make me promise that we would never be him."

"So far it looks like you've succeeded," I tell Adam, but I don't say a word about Scott, because I'm still not sure of his involvement with Teddy.

"The last time I saw my dad he called me a loser." Adam huffs another unamused laugh. "I don't ever seem to live up to my mom's expectations either."

The more I get to know Adam, the more I'm realizing Scott really was the only positive thing in his life. And I took it from him. I owe Adam more than helping him dispose of Ted Lowman's body. I owe him whatever he needs. My actions have caused this boy to be alone in the world.

"I didn't live up to my mom's expectations either," I tell him. "She died thinking I was a disappointment."

Adam snaps surprised eyes to mine. "Then your mom was an idiot because I think you're pretty great."

Despite the odd direction this conversation has turned and the peculiar connection we seem to be developing, I still smile. "I've never admitted that to anyone before."

"It's what happens when you grow up with a powerful parent. They mold you, you try your best to make them proud, and nothing is ever good enough. My dad wasn't powerful, not like Mom, but he was mean. Scott tried to take it all so I wouldn't get it—"

And then I went and accidentally killed him.

"—Like I'm sure you do with your younger sister and brother. You try to protect them."

Yes, Adam is perceptive. I will give him that much.

Another car pulls into the parking lot and Adam finally rounds the back of his old Chevy, heading to the driver's side. "Anyway, I guess I just wanted to make sure you know we're in this together. Whatever happens."

14

FTER MY SHIFT at Patch and Paw, I pull up outside the Youth Center where Justin attends summer camp. I park in an available spot, pull the emergency brake, and right as I climb out, I catch sight of a man sitting over to the left at a picnic table tucked up under the trees.

Looking like a "dad" in jeans, t-shirt, flip-flops, and a baseball cap, he sits alone on one side of the table, his feet planted on the ground and his arms propped on top with a phone held in his hands. To any onlooker he's seemingly looking at his phone, possibly scrolling Facebook, Instagram, or the like.

To any onlooker, but I'm not just any onlooker and my senses prick to instant alert.

I follow his line of sight and the direction his phone points all the way across the grass and over to the playground attached to the Youth Center. The playground where the kindergarten and first-grade students currently play.

Son of a bitch.

Without another thought, I jump from the Jeep, slam my door shut, and stroll straight toward him. His focus stays solely on the phone and when I slide into the bench opposite him, blocking his phone from the playground, he jumps a little and glances up.

"Which kid is yours?" I ask.

A tentative smile dances across his lips. "Um, none actually."

The idiot doesn't even have the wherewithal to lie. My gaze travels over his green baseball hat, his oily nose, and down across his thin upper body before coming back to meet his dark eyes. "Then you need to move," I tell him.

His tentative smile turns into one big, fake, and bright one. "Why? It's a free world and all that."

Reaching forward I pluck the phone right from his fingers and turn it around. He reaches for it. "Hey!"

I want to jab the heel of my hand straight into the tip of his oily nose, but I refrain and instead level him with a dark gaze. Apparently, he realizes I'm not messing around and actually holds his hands up, glancing hesitantly at the phone.

I bring it up in front of my face, keeping partial focus on him, and begin scrolling through the pictures he just took of the playground and the kids. I don't bother finishing because this man is so done.

"D-do I know you?" he cautiously asks.

My dark gaze moves from the phone back to his wormy eyes. "No, and you don't *want* to know me." I lean closer, and he has the smarts to tilt back. "I am here every day, and if I ever see you again, I will not be this nice."

A terrible fake laugh comes out of him. "Y-you've got the wrong idea."

Lightning quick I jab the heel of my running shoe into

the top of his right flip-flopped foot and cram my thumb into the ulnar nerve on his forearm. He gives a satisfactory cringe. "Listen, asshole, I know who you are." I apply more pressure to both points, and he hisses in a breath, trying to pull away.

"I'm different now," he whimpers. "I did my time. You all aren't allowed to do this."

He must think I'm a cop or something. Fine by me. I give him a sharp intimidating leer. "From the outside, you look normal, but you haven't changed. You are who you are."

His bottom lip quivers. "My brain isn't flawed. I can control my compulsions. My past is not a prologue for the future."

Sounds like he's quoting something a counselor told him. I release my hold and stand up, taking his phone with me. "If I ever see you around again, I won't stop with a couple of harmless pressure points."

"But my phone," he blubbers.

I smack him across the face with it, ignoring his yelp, and walk off. *My brain isn't flawed. I can control my compulsions. My past is not a prologue for the future.*

His words ring a little too true for me. Except I would never hurt a child. If I had the time, I'd follow this pedophile and get more information. Really teach him that lesson I threatened. But I have other things to deal with right now, like picking up Justin and looking further into this serial strangler thing.

Plus, I do have Mr. Pedophile Oily Nose's phone, which means I have his contacts and personal information. I can easily find him if I want to.

15

THAT NIGHT AFTER dinner I'm in my room scrolling my laptop, digging for information on the three strangled girls. They're all between the ages of sixteen and nineteen, all petite, and all with long dark hair. There is no mention of the scarf detail and if it weren't for Adam, I still wouldn't know that fact. Ted Lowman was accused of doing girl number one, which is how he came to be on my radar. Now, though, I'm not so sure.

That's not to say he wasn't guilty of something, just not murder. I've got two bodies now—Teddy and Scott. Teddy, the man who lived in his dead granny's house and partied with a bunch of high school and college kids, and Scott, the guidance counselor with the knife.

Teddy and Scott were connected on a deeper level than everyone else is seeing. I just have to figure out how. By now Teddy's house has been turned inside out, and if anything suspicious was found, it wouldn't be released yet because he's still "at large" and the D.A. would be holding her cards close on that one.

My phone rings and I check the display. The area code is here, but I don't immediately recognize the number. "This is Lane," I answer.

"Hey, it's Adam."

I don't bother asking him how he got my number.

"Can we meet?" He asks.

"When?"

"Now. I'm at my brother's place."

"Everything okay?"

"No." Adam quickly rattles off the address to an apartment community, and I grab my keys and am gone.

Scott Butler's place. The man was twenty-six years old, and though Adam didn't specify, I assume Scott lived alone. I wonder if his mom has gone to the apartment yet.

I want to say no because when my mom died, it took months before Victor worked up the courage to clear her things out. For now, I bet the D.A. is keeping her distance from Scott's place. This is probably the first time Adam has been there, and I'm more than curious to see what is there.

SCOTT BUTLER LIVES in an apartment complex in Loudoun County. I pull in and around back to building C, then head up the inside steps to number ten. Adam must be looking out the window for me because he opens the door as soon as my feet hit the landing.

"Has your mom been here too?" I ask, and he shakes his head.

Good, it'll give me a chance to look around. I step inside and my gaze quickly touches on the key features—the flat screen television; the brown leather couch; the kitchen to the right with stainless steel appliances; and the open door straight ahead that leads into a bedroom.

Other than magazines spread across the coffee table, it appears clean and organized.

Without saying a word to me, Adam walks over to the cabinet below the T.V. and pushes the door. It swings open and he rolls out a drawer with neatly filed DVD movies. Curious, I move in and watch as he picks up one with a Hot Tub Time Machine cover. He opens it and shows me the silver DVD with the word *Samantha* printed in black sharpie.

He does the same to Animal House, opening it and showing *Brittanie* printed on that one. Another, this one Old School, opens it to reveal *Joanna* printed on that one. On and on he goes, opening all of the movie cases and finding each with a silver DVD and a different printed girl's name on it.

No wonder he called me. "Have you watched any?" I ask.

Adam shakes his head. "I can't. I'm afraid of what I might find."

I nod. I get that. "Did you call your mom?" I hope not. I want this all to myself.

"No." He pushes to his feet. "I'm going to go for a walk. Will you watch a few and tell me what's on them?"

I try not to show how excited this makes me. "Of course."

With a nod, he steps around me, crosses the living room and without another word, leaves me alone.

I pull a pair of gloves from my back pocket and slip them on, then I grab the one labeled *Samantha* and slide it into the DVD player. It takes me a second to get everything turned on and working, and onto the screen flashes a giggling girl who I assume must be Samantha. She's naked, rolling around on the bed with an equally naked Scott. I take in the surroundings and surmise this was filmed at Teddy's granny's house. More giggling, more rolling around, then sex. I fast forward and that's it. Sex.

I take out *Samantha* and pop in *Brittanie*. But this one features Teddy, not Scott, and again was filmed at Granny's home. I fast forward through all the sex, come to the end, and that's it.

I take *Brittanie* out and slide in *Joanna*. Again filmed at

Granny's, but this one features both Scott and Teddy doing a very willing and enthusiastic Joanna. I fast forward and other than a crotch shot I seriously can do without, there's nothing here.

I keep taking out and putting in new DVD's and they are all the same. Scott, Teddy, young willing girls, and sex. Teddy and Scott may not have been guilty of murder but they were certainly guilty of sex with a minor. I would bet anything some of these girls are from the high school where Scott used to be a guidance counselor.

The verdict is out on why Scott was at Teddy's house that night I accidentally stabbed him, but I would guess it has something to do with these DVD's. One of them probably threatened the other and they got in a stupid fight involving a knife. A fight I then interrupted.

The apartment door slivers open. "Can I come back in?"

I turn off the T.V. "Yes."

Adam hesitantly steps back inside and closes the door. "Well?"

"Sex. Your brother, young girls, and Ted Lowman. That's it."

It takes Adam a second to process that. "Please tell me they weren't raping the girls."

"No." I quickly assure him. "The girls were willing, and by the way they made eye contact with the camera, I'd say they also knew they were being filmed."

Closing his eyes, Adam blows out a relieved breath. "Guess that explains why Scott was at Ted Lowman's house that night."

"Yes."

Adam notes the gloves I slipped on and smiles a little. "Good thinking."

"I wasn't sure if you wanted to leave the sex tapes or dispose of them?"

"Leave them. It'll be interesting to see what Mom does with all that."

Yes, it will, and I don't question Adam's decision because clearly there are some family dynamics that he's working through. I more than get that.

Adam sits down on the edge of the couch. "Actually, I know her, and she won't look for Ted Lowman after finding these videos. She'll do everything she can to cover this up."

I have to say, Adam impresses me because I do believe he's on to something. These sex tapes just might be our key to getting the D.A. off the missing Teddy case. "You're a smart guy, Adam."

He blushes a little, and something shifts inside of me, a sense of protectiveness that wasn't there before, and I wonder if he ever hears praise. "I can tell you're uneasy with compliments. It's okay. We all want to be liked. It's human nature." Well, for everyone but me. I could care less if people like me.

Adam's face gets a little redder. "This, um, seems odd for you, talking to me like this. You always seem so cautious with your words, like your guard is up. I wish I had that trait."

It's not a trait. It's my nature. Yet somehow that guard he's talking about has lowered a bit with him. I never take sides, but I'm finding myself on Adam's side in all of this, and I'm not sure what to think about that. I like Adam, and whether I want to admit it or not, we are linked by a series of events. On some level, I do trust him.

Or maybe I'm being foolish.

He stands up. "Well, anyway, you've done a lot for me, and if I can ever repay the favor, don't hesitate to ask."

"Okay," I say, immediately taking him up on that. "I want to know about the three strangled girls. I want to know everything you can get me on the cases."

Adam surprises me when he doesn't hesitate either. "Done."

I open the door to leave, a slight smile on my face until he says, "Actually...no. These sex tapes are not how Mom should remember Scott, and I should be ashamed for thinking that way."

Slowly, I turn, my smile sliding away. Not only is Adam too good, but he also doesn't realize what he's saying. The sex videos are the key to getting the D.A. off our trail.

Adam starts taking the DVD's out of the entertainment center, and I know I need to move fast. I step forward. "Why don't you let me take care of those?"

He glances up, and behind his glasses relief flashes through his light brown eyes. "Really?"

I nod, ignoring the guilt that flares through me. "Really."

17

WITH SCOTT'S SEX-CAPADES in a box in the back of my Jeep, I pull up outside the house where I'm supposed to pick up Daisy. She has her driver's license now, but no wheels, and where I used to mind the whole chauffeur thing, it's not so bad anymore.

She's standing with a group of her girlfriends, laughing and talking. I study her for a few seconds and something seems off. This isn't the Daisy I saw earlier. Where this morning her demeanor was relaxed and approachable, now it comes across haughty and very "mean girl".

She catches sight of me then, leans in to say something to her friends, to which they all snort and giggle, then trots across the yard toward me. Opening the passenger door, she climbs in and drops her purse in the floorboard. Then she shuts her door and clicks on her seatbelt.

I put the Jeep in gear and pull away. "What are you doing?"

"What do you mean?"

"Back there. That wasn't you." It was the person that she used to be but not the person she is now.

Leaning over, she grabs a chapstick from her purse and slicks it across her lips. "I'm role-playing."

Role-playing? What the hell does that mean?

"It's just easier," she says, "then showing them the real me."

Holy shit. That hits way too close for comfort. "I get that," I carefully say, wanting to know how long exactly she's been doing that. "And who is the real you?"

She shrugs. "Who knows?"

After Mom died, I found a box that I'm positive she never intended me to uncover. Inside were gruesome pictures of her and my birth father cutting people up. Aunt Marji was in some of them, too. As disturbing as it was to find those, what I uncovered at the bottom sent me into a tailspin.

I found an envelope from a lab with evidence that Daisy was their child too. She is not Victor's daughter and my half-sister, as I always thought. She is, in fact, my real sister.

When I found this out, I promised myself I would be there for her. I would watch. I would listen. I would guide her to a more positive path. But at this moment, I don't know what to say. She sounds just like me when I was her age.

So I do the only thing I can, I remind her of what I've said before. "Always remember you can talk to me about anything. No judgment. And no matter how odd or strange your thoughts, I'm always here for you. I promise you that."

But Daisy doesn't answer, doesn't even nod, and instead turns to look out the passenger window. I glance at her pretty profile and at her blonde hair blowing with the night breeze. She really does look most like Mom. Sometimes it's hard to look at Daisy and not immediately think of our mother.

Something is definitely going on in Daisy's head. I can

keep reassuring her and encouraging her to talk, but I highly doubt she will. It's going to take me opening up about my own darkness to give her the freedom to do the same.

I just don't know if I'm ready for that.

Big sister, loving daughter, friend to Adam, works at an animal clinic... These all sound so normal and upstanding. So harmless and much better than the girl who keeps to herself and only plays with Corn Chip. Yes, these all sound so real and loving, but do I genuinely feel them? Have I spent my entire life role-playing and I don't even realize it?

Maybe I should take my cue from Daisy and really throw myself into the various roles, and even expand on them. Maybe I should throw "girlfriend to Tommy" into the mix, though I'll have to think on that one for sure.

18

"IT'S ANOTHER WORTHLESS tip," District Attorney Butler tells my stepdad, her voice coming through the speaker on his cell. "But I'll chase every single one of them until I find Scott's killer."

"What can I do?" Victor asks, moving to shut the office door and muting their conversation.

I stand in the kitchen, cutting vegetables for our dinner salad and, of course, eavesdropping. Another worthless tip. Thanks to me. I called in an anonymous tip that Ted Lowman had been sighted down in Richmond. I have a theory that if I keep Butler and her team running in circles, then they won't have time to make any real connections.

In my Jeep still sits the box of sex movies that will most definitely divert her attention, but I'm trying to be a good friend to Adam. Turning over a new leaf and all. Yet I'm so good at inciting. It's my strong point.

The D.A., though, she's obsessed. As I would be if someone had killed Victor or Daisy or Justin. So I get it. I do. She's not going to stop looking until she finds a viable reason to put this thing to bed.

Adam's words come back to me—*let's just tell her*—and I briefly entertain that idea. Grief has hit the D.A. hard and she wants justice. Would she really accept the fact Adam killed Ted Lowman? Would she consider it justice and put the topic to rest, or would she consider it a criminal act and go after her own son?

I don't know. It's a big secret to keep and Adam is right there living with her, day in and day out. If he cracks, we're both going down. I have to make sure he doesn't break under pressure. I have to make sure he keeps stable. Let the D.A. be the troubled one.

Adam needs to know this is my burden, too. He's not alone. Whatever decision is made should come from both of us. Frankly, he needs to know and realize I'm uncomfortable. That I may seem like the level-headed one, but I'm not.

Adam thinks this will all die down. Not a chance. None of this is going away. The D.A. is like a dog with a meaty bone. Adam needs some new perspective, some reassurance, and perhaps to be reminded that his kill was done with intent. Even if he doesn't want to admit it.

Role-playing. Yes, it's time for me to be a bit more dramatic with Adam. Not so even-keeled. Let him be the one to see reason.

Daisy laughs, bringing me from my thoughts, and I glance through the kitchen and into the living room where she and Hammond are snuggling on the couch. Is she role-playing or is that true love? I try to imagine me and Tommy there, snuggling, laughing. The scene filters through my thoughts, not entirely uncomfortable.

Hm, interesting.

Maybe role-playing falls more into two categories: character actors and leads. Leads would be exhausting, I think, with all those emotions. Yes, there's something to be said for being the character actor. Between Daisy and me, she's the lead for sure. I wonder if all that emotion exhausts her.

But if she can be that convincing, surely I can too.

Victor comes from the office and into the kitchen, opening the refrigerator and grabbing bottled water. He uncaps it and takes a swig before crossing over to the counter and peeking over my shoulder. "Radishes?"

I shrug. "Thought I'd try something new."

He snatches a cherry tomato and pops it into his mouth.

"Dad?"

"Hm?"

I nod into the living room and to Daisy and Hammond. "How do you know when you're in love?"

He doesn't immediately answer, which means he's either thinking, or he's never been in love and doesn't know how to answer. Either way, I glance his way to see him watching my sister and her boyfriend, too.

He swallows his cherry tomato. "Something inside of you recognizes the other. It's when you don't feel alone anymore in the world. Like your life is no longer an unanswered question. You feel real."

Huh. I think back through the years and to all the people I've met, and the only ones I've "recognized" or felt a connection to were the ones hiding something. I'm not sure what to think about that.

"Do you feel alone now that Mom's gone?" I hope not. Victor is one of my favorite people. I only want everything good and right for him.

He slings his arm over my shoulders. "With you three kids, I'm good."

I give him a little smile, but I want more for him. I want him to have someone great. I don't want Mom to be the "love of his life". He deserves better.

He says, "Also, and this is probably the information I'll give Justin one day, women lead with their hearts. It's a good thing to remember during the wooing stage."

Women lead with their hearts. I never once have. But if that's true, then the D.A. is definitely not letting Scott's death go.

19

"I DON'T KNOW what's going on," Adam whispers into the phone later that night. "People are calling in that they've seen Teddy."

Internally, I smile. "Huh, that's weird."

"And every time a new one comes in, Mom gets even more riled up."

"Yeah, I did overhear a conversation between her and my dad."

"What did you overhear?"

I decide to embellish. "'Expansion of the task force. All hands on deck. If it's the last thing she does.' Those type of things."

Adam blows out a long and frustrated breath.

"I'm sure it'll die down," I lie. "She'll eventually accept the loss and move on."

"Nobody's moving on," Adam mumbles. "I keep trying to make some sort of connection with her over Scott's death, but everything I say seems to upset her more." Through the phone, I hear him shift and think he must be putting me to the other ear. "Ya know, I used to think people were either good or bad, but now I think there are good people that do bad things."

Maybe he's talking about the fact that his brother had sex with teenage girls. I wonder if I should tell Adam I dry humped Dr. Issa to give him some perspective on the age thing. Or perhaps he's talking about the fact that he killed Teddy.

"Everyone does have a dark side," I assure him.

"I know you don't want to hear this, but I really do think Mom will be okay if I just come clean to her. I hate liars, and now I am one."

I don't know why he keeps trying to cast his mom in this understanding role. The D.A. will not be okay with this information. "Adam, you need to promise me that you'll keep your mouth shut. This isn't just you that we're talking about. This is me, too."

"I know," he sighs. "I know. I promise."

Now would be a good time to remind him of some well-placed sex tapes, and his mom will divert this whole thing for good.

"It's just...she's never been proud of me," he quietly admits. "I used to tell myself I didn't care because I always had Scott. But now he's gone, he's left me alone, and like it or not Mom is the only thing I have left. She's my only connection."

I get the whole connection thing, the whole loneliness thing. It's hard to find someone, and it can be cumbersome keeping secrets. I get that. "Well, you've now got me," I say, surprised to truly mean it.

Though I can't see his face, I feel his smile through the phone. "Thanks."

This isn't playing out as I thought. I riled things up with the anonymous tips, thinking it would convince Adam to deliver the sex tapes, but it's only making him want to come clean to his mom even more than before.

Yes, I was hoping to get his go-ahead with the tapes, trying to be a good friend and all, but now I see that's not going to happen.

Emotional intelligence leads to more success than anything measured on a standard IQ. I read that somewhere, and I need to remember that because I'm definitely lacking in emotional intelligence and my new friend, Adam, seems to have it in abundance.

For that matter, so did my mom. That's why she was so successful at being the evil that she was and getting away with it for so long. She had a lot of tools in her box—Mom, wife, FBI, community leader—and a fabulous poker face. Yes, Mom knew how to roleplay, just like Daisy.

Damn, I don't like thinking like that.

Going with the role-playing, I decide to switch roles with Adam. "Maybe you're right...maybe we should tell your mom."

Through the phone, his voice brightens. "Really?"

I don't like that I've made him so excited, but it is what it is. "Really."

"This is good. Mom's in a lot of pain, and this will end it."

He thinks he's going to be her golden child now.

"Plus, she'd never jeopardize her career by prosecuting me, or rather us."

Sadly, she probably would. If there's one thing I've noticed about the D.A., she's hard, but she also loves a good spotlight. Imagine the press she'd get over prosecuting her own son for the murder of the murderer of her other son. That's a mouth full, but it would make the national spotlight.

However, those sex tapes of her murdered son with minors? Oh, hell no. She'll go to the ends of the earth to cover that one up and anything linked to it. That would put her in a spotlight for sure, and not the type of spotlight she wants.

I like Adam and I take no pleasure in manipulating him this way. Still, I say, "Okay, but we do it together."

First, though, I plan on sending the D.A. a little package.

20

THE NEXT EVENING I ring the bell on the Butler's McMansion, ready to play this thing out, and the door swings open before the gong has completed.

Adam spares me one slight glance as he slips outside, closing the door behind him. I take a step back, sensing something's off. I'm curious to see how he's going to respond to the recent delivery.

With a sigh, he steps down the porch and idly wanders off into the side yard. Silently, I follow.

He comes to a stop in the grassy side yard and takes a moment to look across the wide expanse of their property. On the distant horizon, the sun dips, almost ready to set and cast us into darkness. If there's one thing I have, it is patience, and I use it while I wait for him to speak.

He nods to the bordering woods. "Scott and I used to play G. I. Joe in those woods." He points to a hill in the distance. "We used to sled that in the winter and set up a water slide in the summer. Me and Scott, we always had each other. We knew each other inside and out." Adam huffs an unamused laugh. "Or at least I thought I did."

I wait for him to say more, but he doesn't. Scott was obviously the favorite of their mom and just as obvious, Adam holds resentment over that. Adam may love Scott, but he can still be envious of him.

I was clearly the favorite of my mom, and it never occurred to me until just now, but Daisy may have been jealous of that. "I've never had that," I tell Adam. "Someone who knew me inside and out." Well, except for Mom, but she doesn't count. Nothing about her counts.

"Then I guess you're lucky because you don't know what it's like to lose it. I lost my dad a long time ago to alcohol. I lost my mom to her career. And now I've lost Scott. I have to figure out a way to fill those holes." Adam shifts away from looking at the setting sun to looking at me. "I've been fooling myself. I can't trust Mom with my secret. Our secret."

This is what I wanted, but I'm confused. Does he not know about the package I anonymously sent his mom?

"Really right now there's only one person I can trust, and it's you. Except... I get the impression our secret isn't your only secret."

Wow, um, okay, Adam really is observant, and I'm both comforted by that and uneasy with it. "Everyone's got secrets."

"Sure I get that." His expression becomes somber. "But it's a burden to keep those secrets, yeah?"

I don't respond, because he's right, it is a burden.

"Maybe we can share each other's load." Adam turns back to the house. "Just think about it." He paces away and turns to gaze at me over his shoulder. "I get why you sent the sex tapes to my mom. It really was the best way to get her to drop the search for Ted Lowman. But let's make that the last secret we keep."

I came here ready to play dumb. Ready to lie, to weave a tale about someone else knowing about those videos and sending them in, but as I stand here looking at Adam, I know without a doubt he'll see right through me, and I'm not sure why, but that matters. "So I take it the delivery worked?"

"Yes, Mom has completely diverted the whole thing. She's putting all of her energy and resources into The Strangler."

"That's good," I assure him.

He nods. "I guess I'll see you around."

Adam walks off, and I stand in his side yard watching him the whole way, weighted with our conversation and my deceitful actions. I tell myself everything I've done is justified, but somewhere deep in my gut I know I'm lying.

Remorse—it's a foreign feeling, and for the first time in my life, I want to make it up to him. I want to be deserving of Adam's trust.

Plus, now is probably not the best time to ask him about The Strangler information he was going to get me.

21

FROM ADAM'S I go straight to Tommy's place, spy his bike in the usual spot, and park my Jeep and climb out.

Friends, family, boyfriend. If you roleplay long enough, does the whole thing become real? Does Daisy roleplay because she thinks it will make *her* real? It's an interesting thought, and one I want to explore. If Tommy will let me.

His door swings open, and I note his wet hair and shirtless tattooed body. I've never seen his bare upper body and my eyes widen appreciatively. I mean, I've obviously felt it through his T-shirt, and I know he's tone, but to see said toneness? Not bad.

Not bad at all.

I don't bother disguising my hungry gaze as it travels over his curved biceps, his pecs dusted with a bit of blonde hair, and down to his defined stomach. The waistband of his jeans rides low on his hips and I want to put my lips right there where those dips are in his hips.

Tommy laughs. "Lane?"

I take a step forward. "Holy shit, you're hot."

He grabs my forearm and tugs me in, and I land solidly against his equally solid chest. His soapy shower smell surrounds me as he goes in for a kiss, not shy about grabbing my ass and squeezing.

I kick the door closed, not breaking lip contact, and he unsnaps and unzips my jeans. Then they're down my legs. Then they're off. Then he's hoisting me up onto the kitchen island. Then his mouth travels down my body and he "returns the favor" he promised the last time I was here.

Afterward, he grabs me another lime Jell-O, and we park it side-by-side on his couch. Several long minutes go by as we slurp our Jell-O, and I conjure up every position I want to try with this guy.

After my mind combs through them all, it starts backtracking through all the conversations Tommy and I have had. I think of that time he broke down on the Parkway and called me for a ride. We talked about connecting with someone, being real with someone. That conversation closely parallels the one I had earlier with Adam.

I think there are a lot of people out there looking for that connection. That one person you can trust with your secrets. That one person who won't judge. The question is, how do you know who that one person is?

If I ever told Tommy the real identity of the Decapitator, that my mom was the actual person who killed his sister, he'd throw me out. There's no way he could handle that truth. Just like there's no way Adam could handle the truth that I am the real person who killed his brother. Albeit accidentally, but still it happened.

Maybe I could share some things with Tommy and other things with Adam. Perhaps that's more what connecting is about. You share certain things with certain friends and other things with other friends. Who knows?

It probably is easier to keep things to myself.

My copycat, Catalina, insisted Tommy was hiding something. She could've been playing me by saying that. I don't know. But as I turn and look at Tommy, I can't help wondering if he has these same thoughts. Does he want to share his secrets with me?

Grabbing the remote, he flips on the T.V. before grasping my legs and swinging them over his lap. I go with the gesture, relaxing back on his couch, falling into the sensation of him stroking my bare ankle.

I take a second to look more closely at his tattoos, remembering that he said they are from his sister's paintings. I don't know anything about art, but from the forms and colors, I think she must have dabbled in abstract pieces.

My eyes travel over his still bare chest and what I really want to do is get completely naked, but I push that down and concentrate on making a connection instead.

I clear my throat. Here it goes. "My whole life has always seemed like a bunch of questions that needed to be answered. Like I've always been waiting for something to happen to make sense. Lately, I've been thinking about the word connection and thinking I need to make one. A real one with someone. I mean, not just someone, *you*." I clear my throat again. "That is if you'd be open to that."

Tommy mutes the already quiet T.V. and shifts a little, so his body points toward mine. "Are you asking me to be your boyfriend?"

I think about that a second. "I don't know. Am I?"

His lips tilt up a bit on one corner. "Yes, I think you are."

I keep going, figuring why stop now? "The thing is, you make me feel real. And while I love the lime Jell-O and the fooling around, I also would love to, I don't know, maybe go on an actual date?"

I try to imagine me and Tommy sitting across from each other at a romantic restaurant and no, that doesn't seem right. I think we're more of a pizza here at his apartment kind of couple. "I think I'm botching this up. I've only been on one other date and that was hockey and hotdogs with Zach." And, wow, that's a name I haven't thought of in a while. "Zach and I had sex in my bedroom. I also dry-humped his older brother, Dr. Issa." I cock my head. "I don't think I'm supposed to say all of that to you, am I?"

Tommy starts laughing, and he doesn't stop.

"What?" I ask.

He rubs his eyes, shaking his head, still laughing. "God, Lane, you are the weirdest girl."

"Thank you?"

Tommy glances at me, laughter dancing across his face. "Yeah, you're weird, but seeing you is always the highlight of my week. Whether you know it or not, I'd already decided to hang on to you for a bit. I figured you'd come to that conclusion eventually."

"So are you saying yes to the dating thing?" I clarify.

He grabs the front of my shirt and tugs me forward. "Yes, I can get into the boyfriend-girlfriend thing. Let's do this."

I give him a solid kiss, my way of saying yes, too. Role-playing, acting, the arts. Most creative people toil with their talents, perhaps never stepping into the spotlight. But if you focus and study your craft, you might just get that big break.

I'd like to think I just made a steady effort in fine-tuning my role-playing craft.

H OW MANY TIMES have I sat here in Judge Penn's court? The smell of cleaning products lingering. My favorite vent directly above me always blowing cold air. The sound of his gavel determining the direction of a person's life.

My sanctuary.

But are these times almost gone? How can I just pick up and move to UVA? This is my home. It's going to be hard to find another Judge Penn.

Innocent until proven guilty. It's a holistic approach and one I don't subscribe to. I've been hanging out in Judge Penn's courtroom for years, and though I've never personally met him, I think he and I might be friends. He seems like he would enjoy handing out tough sentences if only the law would let him.

Jurisdiction issues, fancy lawyers, evidence mishandling...there are too many people who skirt by, which is where I come in.

I've met many a friend in Penn's courtroom. Like The Weasel, the rapist; Aisha, the drug dealer; Ted Lowman; and now Mr. Oily Nose, the pedophile. That's right, me and Oily Nose meet again. Last I saw him he wore a baseball hat and now I discover he's got an oily balding head to match his nose.

Judge Penn points his fist. "You listen to me you piece of trash, if I ever see you in here again, I don't care what evidence is or is not admissible, I will take you down. Do you understand me?"

And that right there is why I think Penn and I would be friends.

Mr. Pedophile Oily Nose drops his head, all submissive, and nods his acquiescence. The gavel bangs and Oily Nose exchanges a handshake with his lawyer before turning and walking down the middle aisle that leads out of the fairly empty courtroom.

Usually, I keep a low profile but something drives me to stand, to draw attention to myself. It works because Oily Nose glances up and his eyes widen when he sees and recognizes me. The shock in his expression has me smirking.

That's right, you ass wipe, I'm coming after you.

"Lane?"

I turn a full one-eighty to see Adam standing in the back corner of the courtroom. Pushing his glasses up, he glances at Oily Nose as he exits the back double door, before bringing his curious light brown eyes back to mine. "What are you doing here?"

"Give me a couple of minutes," Judge Penn calls from his bench, before leaving through the side door to where I assume his chambers are.

I turn back to Adam. "How do you know the Judge?"

Adam starts walking toward me. "He's my uncle. We meet for dinner every so often."

Interesting. A mom that's the D.A. and a judge for an uncle. But not just any judge, Judge Penn. The man whose courtroom I have frequented more times than I can count. Because of this, I know I have to tell as close to the truth as possible. Penn saw me and Adam talking. Penn knows I hang out in his courtroom. Penn's staff believes I'm here because I'm interested in law.

"I come here a lot," I tell Adam. "I've never seen you before."

Adam shrugs. "Guess our paths never crossed. What do you mean you come here a lot?"

I shrug, too, all nonchalant. "I'm really curious about the law. I've been in an out of numerous courtrooms, but I like Judge Penn and the way he handles his room."

"I thought you wanted to be a Vet."

Another shrug. "I don't know. I like both. Maybe I'll be an animal rights activist."

Adam smiles a little, and I'm confident he doesn't suspect my motives for being here. "So how long you been standing back there?" I ask.

"Enough to know that man is guilty." Adam glances at the double doors Mr. Oily Nose went through. "I'd love to hand that guy over to the BDAP."

"BDAP?"

"Biker Dudes against Pedophiles."

"That actually exists?"

Adam's dark brows go up. "Oh yeah. It's a badass group of men who lobby against child sex crimes. They travel all over the Nation on their bikes, talking to schools, educating kids, fundraising for victims, organizing rallies, and anything else you can imagine."

How have I not heard of this?

Adam steps in closer, lowering his voice. "But it's the

rumored behind-the-scenes stuff that they're most known for. Justice for those wronged. Good kind of justice if you know what I mean. An eye for an eye type of stuff."

In other words, my kind of stuff.

"Yeah," Adam says, "if I had my way I'd hand that pedophile over to them and let them do their worst, or rather best."

I'm all about letting someone have their way. Seems Adam and I understand each other better than either one of us knows. The judge's hands may be tied, but mine sure aren't. I can do us all a favor because with my brand of justice, I don't compromise.

23

I 'VE BEEN WORKING at Patch and Paw for several years now. I've cleaned cages. Tended wounds. Assisted in surgery. Been there during an animal's last breaths. But I have never in all those years seen a live birth.

Until now.

"There you go, Momma," Dr. O'Neal coos, stroking the Cocker Spaniel's head. She turns to me, beaming. "Incredible, isn't it?"

There's Dr. O'Neal, gushing with emotion over an animal that doesn't even belong to her. I try to imagine Dr. Issa here and how he would react, and he'd do the same thing. I know he would.

Anyone would.

Anyone but me.

I don't feel that runaway emotion. I only feel the Receptionist beside me, clenching my upper arm. At some point during the birth, she grabbed hold of me, and she has yet to let go. She's a tiny woman and stronger than she looks. I want to peel her fingers off my upper arm, but I refrain. Apparently, she needs personal contact, and so I let it be.

I go beyond this scene and back in time to my mom birthing me and Daisy and Justin. Was she overflowing with true emotion, or was she role-playing? I see Victor there, beaming just like Dr. O'Neal currently is, and I see Mom with her pretty smile, hiding her thoughts of inevitability.

She knew she had a role to play, and she played it to a tee.

I keep thinking about those words roleplay—daughter, sister, animal lover, and now girlfriend. I need to get into my role, and I need to maintain it, however exhausting that may be. It's the only way I'm going to fully blend.

So I paste a smile on my face, and I squat down to rub the Cocker Spaniel's head. Life just happened in front of me, and if you really think about the science behind it, it's a truly overwhelming event. The odd thing is, I really do wish I wasn't so indifferent to this amazing scene in front of me. I really do wish I felt something more than the science behind it.

24

"**W**HEN LANE MOVES out, what are we doing with her room?" This is what Justin asks over dinner that night.

I pause in my bite of stuffed cheesy shells and glance first at Victor before my eyes shift over to Justin. "I didn't realize you were in such a hurry for me to go."

"I'm not!"

I go ahead and swallow my bite, then chase it with a quick drink of lemonade. Though I haven't talked to Victor about this, I have been thinking of the whole moving off to college thing. My plan was always to go to UVA, but that would put me hours from here. Hours away from Daisy.

When I first discovered her real parentage, I knew my future would probably change. Now with the brief talks she and I have had, and the glimpses she's given me into her own thoughts, I both want to and know I need to stay closer. I want to be here for her. I want to be close enough to keep an eye on her.

I give my mouth a quick wipe. "What would you all think about me staying local for college?"

Victor glances up from his dinner. "Really? Why?"

"With everything that has happened," I honestly say, "I want to be here for you all."

Daisy perks up, and I'm so glad to see that reaction in her. "Serious?" She grins. "I think that sounds great!"

Justin makes a face. "Dang, I was hoping to snag your room."

Playfully, I push his head. "You little twerp. You can have my room if it's okay with Dad. I'm still planning on getting my own place."

I look across the table at Victor and my smile falls away when I note his none-too-happy expression.

"It's not what your mother would have wanted," he says. "She really wanted you to go to UVA."

I want to reply with, *Who the hell cares what Mom wanted?* But instead, I tactfully say, "Well, it's ultimately my decision, right? I mean, I'm paying for it, and I've already been accepted to several colleges here local. I have until the end of the month to make a switch before my acceptance letters expire."

Victor takes a sip of his red wine, and I recognize the gesture. He's giving himself time to think. I get it. I should have talked to him privately about this instead of springing it on the whole table.

Carefully, he puts his wine back down. "I didn't realize you had applied to other colleges."

"Yes, after Mom died I wanted to have options."

Victor looks around the table, his gaze meeting each of ours. I imagine he feels like a General surrounded on the battlefield. Daisy and Justin are clearly on my side of this, and Victor has no option but to acquiesce.

His eyes come back to mine. "You get something in your

head, and there's no stopping you. You're just like your mother that way."

I hate that he just said that.

"Well, every young person needs their independence and privacy. If you want my help looking for an apartment, let me know, because you and I both know you're not a dorm girl."

Wow, I really hurt his feelings. "Dad, I'm sorry. This was not the way I should have talked to you about this. And, yes, I would like help looking for an apartment." I don't really need the help, but I know I need to let him do this to smooth things over.

Plus, he's right. I'm not a dorm girl. I definitely need my privacy.

"Wait," Daisy says, "aren't you required to live in a dorm your freshman year?"

Shit, she might be right.

25

I MAY NOT have the ability to hack my way through whatever network needs to be hacked, but I have my own ways of finding out things. Like for example I still have Mr. Oily Nose's phone.

It's amazing how many people don't password protect themselves, and it's amazing what people keep on their phones. Numbers, of course. Addresses. Credit card information. Porn apps. Calendar of events. Personal notes. IM messages with other deviants. Pictures of children...

Yes, Oily Nose may be doing a stellar job of skirting the law, but there is nothing innocent about his intentions. And I fully plan on exposing him.

To the right people.

Biker Dudes against Pedophiles does indeed exist with headquarters in Texas and several affiliated clubs across the U.S. One here local in D.C.

Mr. Oily Nose lives in Annandale and according to his schedule, he works Monday through Friday from eight until five as a bank teller. What a nice job.

This is my late morning at Patch and Paw, so I park my

Jeep a block down from Oily Nose's apartment and watch as he leaves in his black pants, white shirt, and blue paisley tie. So respectable. He climbs into an equally respectable Nissan Sentra and pulls away from the curb.

I let a good solid five minutes go by just to make sure he didn't forget anything and decides to come back. Then I jump from my Jeep and stroll the sidewalk straight to his brick apartment building.

I wave hello to one person. Give a kind smile to another. Nothing going on here folks.

There are four units total in the small building. Two on the bottom and two on the top. His sits on the bottom and to the right. I don't even use my lockpicks. The idiot has a hide-a-key behind the lamp attached to the wall in the upper left corner—a detail he notated on his phone. Not a bright guy, this one.

I slip on my gloves, take the key, and walk right inside.

It looks a lot like Scott Butler's place. One bedroom. Neat and tidy. Flat screen. Entertainment center. Carpet. Leather couches. Maybe sexual deviants all have the same tastes.

Oily Nose's blinds lay in an open slit pattern, letting in sunlight. It's enough to see by and I begin my perusal. Bedroom first where I find the standard stuff—clothes, family picture beside the bed, light blue sheets, dark blue comforter, dry cleaning hanging in the closet, shoes lined perfectly, and under his bed a collection of magazine clippings all with children in bathing suits.

His nightly spank bank entertainment, I'm sure.

I take a Ziploc bag from my back pocket and slide all the clippings inside. Bathroom comes next, and after a thorough inspection, it comes up empty of questionable matter.

On to the living room. I flip on the T.V. and begin browsing his recent watch lists and movie purchases. *The*

Human Centipede. The Serbian Film. Irreversible. The Brown Bunny. Lolita...

I can't say I'm surprised.

Unlike in Scott's place, Oily Nose's entertainment center holds no hidden DVD's and other than his questionable tastes in movies, I get nothing.

His laptop, though? A gold mine of pictures he's taken around town, catching children in all sorts of scenarios: playing, crying, running, fighting... There are bookmarked child porn sites, too. Pedophile discussion boards. Saved videos taken right off YouTube. And the motherlode—recordings of him actually speaking to children. How has this guy skirted by the law? One well-placed search warrant and the cops would have everything they need. No wonder Judge Penn is so frustrated.

I click on one of the audio files.

"Well, you're awful pretty," Oily Nose says.

A little girl giggles. "Thank you."

"Is your Mommy here?"

"Yep, just over there."

"Sasha!" A woman's voice yells. "Get over here!"

"Bye!" the little girl says.

"Bye," Oily Nose whispers.

That whisper makes my lip snarl. This bastard is so going down.

I take his laptop and the magazine clippings and truck it back to my Jeep. Those along with his phone are all I need.

26

THAT NIGHT I lay crouched in the back of Mr. Oily Nose's Nissan Sentra, waiting. According to his Outlook Calendar, he was getting home late from work with just enough time to change and head to dinner with friends. A dinner he won't be making it to.

In his rush to get back out the door, I'm counting on him not noticing the missing laptop and magazine clippings.

In my pocket, my cell buzzes and quickly I check the display. Daisy. She'll have to wait. Right now, I need this more than Daisy and her request to pick her up, or drop her off, or grab something on my way home.

It buzzes again, this time Adam. What does he want now? A couple of hours ago he caught me on my way out of Patch and Paw, and I thought that was it.

"Where you headed?" he asked.

"Out with a friend," I lied.

"Oh..." He hesitated. "I was thinking we could grab dinner. Maybe we all could?"

"Ah, well, actually, it's my boyfriend," I continued the lie, *realizing the whole boyfriend thing might pay off in more ways than I realized.*

"Oh, okay, no worries." Adam hesitated again. "Need a recommendation? I know a lot of great places."

"Um, sure."

He proceeded to give me recommendations, and I proceeded to listen. "Maybe we can catch up tomorrow."

"Yeah, sure."

This is the problem with friends. They want to do things, and I want to be right here in the back of this Nissan Sentra, waiting on Mr. Oily Nose.

I wonder how many times my mom crouched in the shadows waiting on her victim. I wonder how many times her cell buzzed with Victor or one of us kids and she ignored it. But even though I'm here and ignoring my family and friends, I'm nothing like her. I have my priorities. But so did she—her priority being her victims. And now here I am doing the same thing. I can have both, though, just like she did. I don't have to choose.

What am I doing? Why am I making comparisons? I am nothing like her, or my real father, or my aunt. Nothing.

My thoughts are interrupted when the locks release. In my pocket, my cell buzzes again, and without looking at it, I power it down. My needy family will have to wait.

The car shifts as Mr. Oily Nose slides in behind the wheel and shuts the door. All kinds of excited nerves snap across my skin and beneath my mask I smile. Oh, we're going to have fun, Oily Nose.

He cranks the engine and chooses a station with classical music.

I sit up in the backseat and slip the noose end of the animal control pole around his neck. This is the first time I've ever used an animal control pole, and I'm excited to see how it will go. The inspiration hit me as I was taking inventory earlier at Patch and Paw, and I felt like I had just discovered a new invention.

One quick yank and the noose settles tight. Oily Nose makes a tiny ratchet of panic, and then that's it.

"All mine," I tell him, and he freezes all neat and perfect, already being a good boy. "You're going to do what I say, right?"

He nods, rasping as his neck pinches with the movement. I glance from the side of his face into the rearview mirror, seeing my own masked face and green eyes. I look into his wide, scared ones, and he says nothing, just stares back, waiting. I pull on the noose again, because I can, and his hand flutters up, not sure if he should fight or acquiesce.

"Be good," I warn.

The fluttering hand falls back down, and I loosen the noose.

He takes in a breath, the air ripping at his throat, and coughs it right back out. The sound of his panic, his submissiveness, only fuels me. "Drive," I instruct.

Mr. Oily Nose stutters into motion and begins to follow directions. He knows I mean business, and I love that. We drive 236 to 395, going straight into D.C. He doesn't object or fight or try to speak, and I find myself wishing he would. This is too easy. He's too nervous. I want him to have hope.

But he keeps both hands on the wheel, his knuckles white, and the rest of his fingers red with blood.

We drive north, the only sounds the soft classical music and the wind whisking by. My gaze drifts briefly to the heavy and full moon, and its solemn glow seems to pulse through my veins. Somewhere deep inside of me, a dark rush of excitement dances.

"Exit here," I say, and his eyes fly to mine, panicked. He

opens his mouth, wanting to speak, and I cut him off
—"Here."

He turns, slumping down like he knows he has no
choice. His car rolls over the pavement, and like a horse, I
pull right on the pole and he follows my lead.

The Sentra exits and then takes a gravel road, barely
visible now in the darkness of night. I've never been here
before but my search said half a mile, a few twists, and then
nothing but the "seedy underbelly" of D.C.

Seedy underbelly. I like that.

But I'm not ready to hand him over to the biker dudes.
Not yet at least. His headlights pick up the remnants of a
crumbling shack. Perfect. "Stop the car," I say.

Oily Nose lurches to obey in a rigid movement driven by
fear. He cuts the engine and everything falls quiet save for
the distant buzz of traffic on 395. Across the street sits a
rundown grocery store, closed for the night and bars on the
window. Next to that lays a park with no grass, two broken
swings, a merry go round tilted off its axis, and one lump on
a bench that I assume is a person. Weeds and unkempt
bushes surround the crumbled shack. A tree lays collapsed
through the ceiling. Other than that, darkness engulfs us.
Perfect.

"Get out," I command.

He doesn't move.

I yank hard on the pole, too hard, and Oily Nose arches
off the seat with a gag.

I put my window down, reach around and open his door,
and then shove him out. He flops to the dirt, and I fling open
my door and have the control pole back in my grip before he
has time to realize I released him.

Darkly, I laugh, tightening my hold again, and I slam my
booted foot down onto his chest.

"I thought I told you to be good." Bending over I stare into his bulging eyes. "You going to listen to me?"

He can't breathe, but he nods his head, and I loosen the noose just a bit. Gasping for air, tears leak from his eyes, but his gaze holds mine with understanding.

"Now get up," I say.

Slowly, his eyes still on mine, he gets up. His whole body trembles as he waits for me to give him the next instruction.

"Inside," I softly say.

Mr. Oily Nose drops his eyes and doesn't look at me again as he starts for the house with me behind him, holding him at length with the animal control pole. He goes obediently, just like a dog, head down, knowing he's defeated.

At the broken door, he stops, and his trembling body transitions into full-on shaking. I give him a prod, then a shove, and he stumbles through the broken door. A quick glance around shows the place filthy, but empty, the roof open to the night sky, the stars above, and that full and fat moon.

A beautiful night for vigilante justice.

I yank on the noose and with a strangled scream he falls to his knees. His fingers grapple at his neck and then with a whimper he covers his face with his hands.

"Do you know why you're here?" I ask.

With a sob, he nods. "Please," he whimpers. "Please, I promise to be good. I promise to stop."

"Stop what?"

But his only answer is another whimper, or more like a whine. A whine that gets on my nerves. I yank hard on the noose before slamming his face into the nasty floor. A bit of blood splatters.

I come down hard, my knee in his back, and I grab the

thinning hair on the back of his head and slam his face down again. More blood splatters.

I get down right in his blubbering face. "You know what I think I'm going to do? I'm going to cut your eyeballs right out so you can't ever look at another child again." I slam his head down even harder. "What do you think about that?"

"No," he cries with his limping tone of voice. "Please. I promise to stop."

"Oh, shut up." I jerk hard on the noose, and he bows off the floor, choking.

"Oh, God," he rasps. "Please."

"That's right, asshole, beg. Beg for mercy."

"Please," he chokes out on a sob. "I only touched them a few times."

What?

He tries to scream, but his throat won't let him. He snivels and cries, snot smearing with the blood and the dirty floor. His bladder lets go, and I climb off of him. I've had enough. I pull him up to his feet.

"I couldn't help myself," he snivels. "You don't understand."

"You're right I don't," I reply, not even recognizing my own voice. It's deeper, darker, almost as if it isn't even me speaking.

He must recognize it, too, because he freezes in place.

I hold the pole steady, staring at his dirty and tear streaked terrified face. "No, I changed my mind. I do understand. Because I can't help myself either." Simultaneously, I yank the noose and kick his feet, and Oily Nose lands in another sprawl on the nasty floor. "The difference is, you can't help yourself with children and I can't help myself with you."

Leaning down, I grab a red brick, and I hold it hovered

above him. Does he see me in my mask and dark clothes about to deliver justice, or does he see all those children he's watched, he's touched, he's talked to? I hope he sees the monster in himself and imagines what is about to happen.

I slam the brick into his jaw, sideswiping so his head snaps in the opposite direction. It does the trick and he blacks out.

I'm not taking this guy to BDAP, I'm doing him all on my own. "Let's see how easy it is to touch another kid with ten broken fingers."

Something soft slides through me then, bringing me to a pause and warming me with the realization that I want to make this special.

Carefully I lay his right phalanges out, spreading them all pretty. Then I take the brick, and I slam those fingers over and over and over again, savoring the release pounding through my body until they lay at twisted angles with jutting bones and torn muscles.

His left hand comes next, and when I'm done, all of his fingers look exceptionally dead.

"And those eyes," I whisper. "You'll never see another child again."

From my cargo pocket, I take a small knife, and I slide it down into and around the socket. The knife comes into a slight resistance of membrane, and I pop out first his right eye and then his left. Other than a slight squelching, the removal of the eyeball makes no sound.

Consciousness comes back to him in a sudden and quick flash. His mouth opens, trying to form a scream, then just as quickly he loses consciousness again. Too bad. I was hoping to see his reaction.

Taking the brick, I smash each eyeball, making sure reattachment is not possible. Then I remove the animal pole and noose, leaving him sprawled on the dirty floor, broken and bloody. I'm not tying him up. I want him running out of this place—blind, broken fingers, bloody, and screaming.

If someone were to walk in right now, they would think *I* am the sociopath, the demon, the monster. They would think *I* am the sick and twisted one. But it's not me, it's him. It's him.

Back outside, I rotate my neck and roll my shoulders, feeling better than I have in a very long time. Relaxed even. Tired. Like my hydraulics have been released. Not a single soul exists out here, only that same body passed out on the bench in the desolate park.

I take everything out of the Nissan that I had planned to give the BDAP. I'd rather leave it here for the cops to find, but this is a bad neighborhood and I don't want to risk things getting stolen. I'll mail it to the cops instead in a neat little package so they know exactly what Mr. Oily Nose has been up to.

Taking my mask off, I tuck it down inside the cargo pocket on my left thigh and carrying the laptop, I make my way down the dark and empty street and several blocks over where I know a Metro stop sits.

I've been through a lot of changes lately, and it's important to take time for oneself. It's healthy to do so, to savor those moments when all feels right in the world. When the universe balances once again. I like knowing I'm part of that balance. I'm part of something bigger than myself.

I ride the Metro from D.C. back to Annandale. It's a long route, but I use the time to drift, to replay and relive every moment with Mr. Oily Nose.

Finally, I'm back at my Jeep and slipping behind the wheel. The phone in my back pocket snags on the seat, and I remember it's there and that I turned it off.

Taking it out, I power up, and seconds later my peaceful and tranquil mood transitions into full-on alarm. Daisy, Justin, and Adam have texted and called me non-stop.

Of the three, I decide on Daisy, and she picks up before the phone has finished its first ring. "Where the fuck are you?"

My jaw clenches. Ever since Mom used that word in the kill room, I hate it. It's the worst word in the world. "I'm in my Jeep."

"Dad had a heart attack. Get here now!"

27

MOM WAS INCAPABLE of compromise. She loved her victims more than her family and in the end, it cost her. I don't ever want to be like Mom, and this right here proves that I can't just do as I please.

I rush into the ER. Adam and the D.A. are the first two people I see. Simultaneously, they stand when they catch sight of me. What are they doing here?

But I don't ask that and instead rush over to the admittance desk. "My dad is here. Victor Cameron."

With a nod, the lady presses a button under her desk. The door behind her and to the right buzzes open, and she says, "Room three."

I hurry through, slipping around a nurse, see room one on the left, room two on the right, around the corner and almost bump into a food cart, and then I catch sight of room three. The door stands open and I stride right in.

Victor lays in a single bed, wires attached to his chest and coming out of his gown and over to a monitor. An IV protrudes from his left hand, pumping in fluids. Daisy and

Justin crowd into the small room, one on each side. Someone must have just asked him something because he shakes his head, or more like wobbles it.

Victor glances over with pain-bleared eyes. He manages a small smile, and that smile hits me solidly in the chest. Pressure nudges at the backs of my eyes, and I'm reminded of the time Mom was in the hospital and I cried. At the time none of us knew she had faked her own stabbing, and I had cried for no reason.

But there is nothing fake about this, and I don't hide the wetness that gathers in my eyes. "I'm so sorry," I mumble. "I had my phone off."

Victor lifts an unsteady hand and with a ragged voice says, "Hey, come here."

I scoot beside Justin and gingerly lay my head on Victor's chest. I listen to his heart beat-beat-beat, and I don't think anything has ever sounded so comforting. He kisses the top of my head, murmuring that it's okay, and I gently press my hand into his side, giving him the best hug I can with all the wires attached.

Behind me Justin scoots in, wrapping his arm around my back and to the left Daisy leans in, too, and my whole family takes a few long seconds to hold each other.

Daisy lifts up first and I meet her eyes, mouthing, *I'm so sorry*. With a tiny smile, she nods, and I know she and I are okay.

I tuck Justin into my side and grasp Victor's fingers, careful of his IV. "What happened?"

"I was over at the Butlers'," he speaks, his voice hazy with medicine. "I collapsed. An ambulance ride later, and here I am."

Well, that explains why the Butlers are here. I look at all

the wires running into the top of his gown. "Daisy said heart attack?"

Victor waves that away with a feeble hand. "A very slight one and nothing anyone needs to stress about."

"Dad," I sigh.

He gives me a tired smile. "I'm on strict orders of a better diet, exercise, aspirin regimen, and general stress reduction."

Victor already eats well and exercises. It's the stress. Between Mom dying, more hours at work, us three kids... I don't know what I'd do if anything happened to him.

That thought barrels into me followed by the distinct realization that it would be all me. If anything happens to Victor, I'm in charge of Daisy and Justin. The only other plausible relative is Gramps, but he's a pain in the ass, and I'm sure as hell not letting Gramps raise Daisy and Justin.

"I was worried when nobody could find you," Victor softly admits.

My hold on his fingers tighten. "I'm here, and I'm not going anywhere. Whatever this family needs, I'll be here." I'll never ignore them again.

"Where were you anyway?" Daisy asks, and I hear the accusation in her tone.

But I don't answer and instead say, "You can't make me feel any worse than I already do." This was a huge wake-up call for me. My life is changing in numerous ways. I'm not going to be like Mom. I'll always put family first.

Victor nods. "Lane's right. Let's move on." His eyes close, and he's clearly floating away into some much-needed sleep.

I nod to the door, whispering, "I'm going to go update the Butlers."

"Come right back," Justin says, and I nod.

Outside in the waiting room, I spy the D.A. standing just

inside the door, talking on her phone. Something must upset her, because she pushes the exit door open and sails through it, her voice carrying back.

Adam sees me and crosses the waiting room to where I stand.

"I should have been here," I tell him.

"It's okay, we all were." He pushes his glasses up. "That's what friends are for."

"Yeah, well, I owe you one." I nod to his mom standing outside. "You should feel free to go. I'm here now, and we'll be okay."

Adam shuffles his feet, glancing down at them and then back up. "Didn't you say you were with Tommy?"

I pause a second, then cautiously say, "Yes."

"That's what I thought, but when we called him, he said he hadn't seen you."

Shit. Who the hell has Tommy's number? "That's right. I got our days mixed up."

"Or maybe you didn't."

My eyes narrow. "What are you trying to say?"

Adam glances at my cargo pants, boots, and black tee. "Interesting outfit."

Yeah, well, I was a little preoccupied when I got the messages Victor was here.

Adam rotates away, his gaze lifting to the television mounted in the corner. The words BREAKING NEWS scroll the bottom. Though the T.V. is muted I watch the scene going on. The yellow police tape. The Nissan Sentra being loaded onto a flatbed. A picture of Mr. Oily Nose flashing onto the screen. In the closed caption box, I catch words like broken fingers and missing eyeballs. Despite the fact Victor is laying in a nearby hospital bed, a thrill still pulses through me at what I did.

"You did that," Adam whispers. "Didn't you? That's where you were."

I roll my eyes off the television and over to Adam. "Do you know how crazy that sounds?"

"You were making sure he could never hurt another child."

I glance around the waiting room, making sure it's empty, before looking back at Adam. "Wasn't me." I turn away. "Listen, my family's waiting."

"It's okay. I'm glad you did it. We're more alike than you think, Lane."

I turn back around. "No, we're not."

"Yes, we are. I would have done the exact same thing, given the opportunity."

"You don't know what you're talking about."

Adam moves in, lowering his voice. "You can be honest with me. I see you. Do you understand? I see you, and I like what I see. You have nothing to be ashamed of, nothing to explain, and nothing to apologize for. I'm with you and your way of thinking. I'm not repulsed by it. I respect it. I support it. One hundred percent."

Then without giving me a chance to respond, he simply glances back up at the television before walking from the waiting room, leaving me standing in a dumbfounded haze.

28

V ICTOR STAYS IN the hospital overnight and the next morning he's home and settled in the recliner reading a book. I make him some herbal tea, Daisy serves him steel cut oats with pecans, and Justin has been running up and down the stairs getting Victor what he needs from his room. If we have our way, he's not moving from that recliner all day.

As I'm wiping down the counters, the doorbell rings, Justin answers, and in walks District Attorney Butler. A few hellos are exchanged and the D.A. comes into the kitchen carrying a casserole dish. We take her a dish when Scott dies, and she brings us a dish for Victor.

It's what people do, exchange food.

With a smile, I take it from her and slip it inside the fridge. Dressed in a skirt and blouse, she wanders into the living room, gives Victor a quick hello hug, and settles daintily on the edge of the couch to talk.

Carefully, I eye them. If she starts talking "shop" with Victor, I'm shutting things down. He needs to rest.

On the counter, my cell buzzes, and I check the display.

It's a text from Adam with a picture of him holding a puppy and a message: I'M OUTSIDE. COME MEET MY NEW FRIEND!

Slipping my phone into my back pocket, I wave Daisy over. "I'm going outside for a few minutes. Do *not* let them talk business. Dad needs peace."

Daisy nods. "Agreed." She waves me on. "I've got this."

I open the door and trot down the few steps, finding Adam off to the right in our side yard. He's sitting in the grass, laughing, rubbing a fuzzy black and brown puppy that looks like a cross between a lab and a shepherd.

Dogs do it to me every time, and smiling I approach. "You could've brought him inside."

Smiling, Adam glances up. "He's a she and she pees everywhere, so no to the inside."

The dog spies me and scrambles over, and I squat down to give her a tickle. She rolls over, squirming and peeing herself, and I chuckle. "What's her name?"

Adam shrugs. "I just got her this morning. The neighbor's dog had a litter a bit ago and had promised one to Scott. It's the only reason why Mom is letting me have her. Though I'm supposed to keep her outside."

I hate the thought of dogs being kept outside, and the next sentences come out of me before I even realize it. "I'll help you put together a good place for her. A nice dog house with comfy quarters. She won't even know she's outside. You've got a great yard, and we can do an invisible fence for her."

Adam brightens. "That sounds great."

Yes, actually it does. I think I could get used to this friend bonding thing.

Moving the pet carrier that he brought out of the way, I lower myself to the grass and I sit cross-legged beside Adam.

I wait for him to bring up yesterday and the words we exchanged in the E.R., but he doesn't.

Instead, we spend a few minutes loving on the puppy like the whole world is okay and right. With the size of her paws and her parentage, she's going to be a big dog. If I had a ball I'd give it a toss to see how the puppy reacts. Some pick up the whole chase-and-retrieve thing automatically and some have no clue. I have a good feeling about this one. I think she'd pick it up quick.

"So, um, Lane. I was wondering if you could tell me how it felt. Ya know when you did what you did to that pedophile."

So much for friend bonding. I don't bother confirming or denying anything and instead say, "Well, you must know. Look what you did to Ted Lowman."

Adam falls quiet, almost like he forgot that whole scene. "But that was more accidental, or rather in the moment. Yours was involved. Planned. Plotted out. You made this world a better place doing what you did. Did it feel right? Did it feel like justice?"

"Yes," I say, now not hiding the fact I stalked and maimed Mr. Oily Nose. "It felt like both of those things."

"Was your sleep afterward restless or good?"

An interesting question. "I slept like a baby."

"Surprisingly I did, too, after Ted Lowman. I heard somewhere that you sleep well when your conscience is clear. Do you believe that?"

"I've heard that, too." Seeing as how I sleep well most of the time, I nod. "Yes, I believe that." But I also remember seeing Adam the day after and his bloodshot eyes. I don't think he slept as well as he says he did. Maybe he's just trying to find common ground to bond.

"I think we could make a good team. We could make a

difference. We could do a lot of things that others can't, like my mom and my uncle. The law doesn't dictate us."

We? Adam thinks he knows me. I suppose on some level that might be true. I helped him dispose of Ted Lowman. He now knows I did the pedophile. Neither thing has made him blink. Except he has no clue what, or rather who, I come from.

Adam wants to understand me. He's trying. But if he really saw the depths and layers, if he really saw what I'm capable of, I'm not sure he would accept it. Some people don't play well with others. I don't connect well with others. But Adam is not going away, as evident by the way he keeps inserting himself into my life. He thinks we're pals. He thinks we're like-minded. Maybe I should put that notion to a test.

Yes, maybe he needs to see firsthand the risks involved. Then he'll rethink this like-minded thing. Just because he killed Ted Lowman in a moment of passion doesn't mean he's cut out for doing it again and again.

Let's see, though. "You said you would get me information on The Strangler?"

Adam nods. "I'm working on it. I promise. I want to check a few things against a national database first."

National database. Well, Adam is proving to be an industrious new friend.

"In the meantime, I have something else in mind."

Something else...okay, clearly he's been thinking about this for a while now. But I'm curious enough to play this out, so I say, "Okay, what do you have in mind?"

The D.A. chooses that moment to make an appearance. "Adam, get the dog and let's go. I have work."

Adam sighs. "See you later."

29

I N THE MEANTIME, *I have something else in mind.*
Adam's words circle through my brain in a constant loop, and I wait for him to contact me. But come the next morning I still haven't heard a word. And while I'm curious to hear what it is he has to say, I'm more curious to find out what he's learned about The Strangler.

Adam has something else in mind, and The Strangler holds my sole focus. This isn't working. I don't like relying on him for the knowledge I want.

I go through the motions of the morning, taking Justin to day camp and dropping Daisy off at Hammond's. I don't work Patch and Paw, and I know Tommy is working a double shift at Whole Foods. Idle hands and all that. I decide to dive into The Strangler. I don't need Adam and his snooping. I've done it before on my own, I'll do it again.

But when I open my email, there's an encrypted message from Adam with a subject line: Check your text for the code to read.

Grabbing my phone, I bring up my texts, finding one from Adam with a code to unlock the message. I like that he's thinking of these things. I type in the code and read the subject line:

THE SOMETHING ELSE...

LANE, this is personal for me.

Her name is Lilith Nealand, and in middle school, she was my best friend. Her older brother was and still is an animal. He stabbed her multiple times with a screwdriver, leaving her a quadriplegic. That was five years ago. This month he was released from prison for good behavior. It didn't take him but a few days to become live online, under a pseudo, bragging in great detail about his sister as well as other things. So much for rehabilitation. I'm attaching the pics and details of the scene. Call me when you're ready to discuss.

AFTER I READ Adam's message, I click on the attached photos and everything inside of me hardens. I stare at the eleven-year-old girl, sprawled on her stomach, her yellow nightgown saturated in blood, darker in the areas where the screwdriver went in.

Carefully, I read the details. She was in bed, heard something in the garage, and went down to see. The stabber brother was there, four years older, anger driving his pacing, picking up small tools, throwing them at the back wall. There was an open toolbox, he spun to grab the next object, caught sight of the sister and lost it. Stabbed her four times. The first one went in her shoulder, causing her to fall to the ground. As she tried to crawl away, he stabbed her three more times in the back, the last one severing her spinal cord and leaving her a quadriplegic.

No one saw it happen but he volunteered this information, blaming it on his girlfriend who had just broken up with him and sent him into a blind rage. The mom is who found the sister, only seconds after it happened.

If the mom would have come down a fraction earlier... If the girl would have stayed in bed... If the brother had only stabbed her three times versus the fatal four...

Timing. What an awful thing.

Next Adam has attached transcripts of chat rooms where Stabber Brother has been active under a pseudo, detailing what it feels like to stab a young girl versus an older boy. So Stabber Brother must have targeted someone else, either before the sister or during his stint in juvie and later prison.

I continue browsing the scripts, my jaw tightening with each detailed sentence. At the bottom, Adam has notated Stabber Brother's IP address and its direct link to his current place of work. There's even a camera shot of him on the computer in the break room. Proof that the pseudo is indeed Stabber Brother and proof that he's an idiot. Doesn't he realize everything's traceable?

Adam's got no argument out of me. Stabber Brother deserves my kind of justice, or *our* kind of justice, according to Adam.

I think, though, that I need to appeal to reason. To let Adam see the downside. Perhaps I need to give enough cons to outweigh the pros. Reason is supposed to lead to self-preservation, isn't it? Enough reason and he'll go back to playing with the puppy and leave Stabber Brother to me.

I compose an email back: *We already "took the garbage out" twice. Let's leave it at that. Quit while we're ahead. We both have too much to lose.*

By "garbage" I, of course, mean Teddy and Oily Nose.

A lot of stretched seconds go by, and I get no response. Good, maybe Adam realizes this isn't for him. But Stabber Brother is definitely for me.

I go to get up and my cell surprises me with a text: I WON'T LET YOU DOWN. ALL WE NEED IS A PLAN.

We. There it is again. I want to tell Adam to get another hobby, that this one is taken, but instead, I go back to looking at the picture of the little girl, face down in a pool of her own blood. Her school pictures are attached, one of her grinning and healthy at eleven and one now at sixteen propped in a wheelchair, her body strapped in and her head tilted back at an odd angle. She's smiling for the camera, but it's a lopsided smile brought on by her paralysis.

The meaning of life. I look at her current picture, and I don't get it. Who would she be right now if circumstances were different? She wouldn't be this shell of herself, that's for sure. Does she ever wish she would've died? Does her mom? Seems like a last breath would be a mercy for this girl. I can't begin to imagine the constant pain she endures, not to mention the loss of dignity.

But the worst part is, Stabber Brother doesn't care.

He's going to care after I get done with him. After *we* get done with him. Because it's clear Adam has been thinking about this for a while now. Whether I like it or not, I'm going to be linked to him on this one, too. Because if I don't take Adam under my wing, he's going to target Stabber Brother on his own.

And my gut tells me, things won't go well. Adam doesn't see it, but he is not ready for that gigantic step.

30

THE COPS RECEIVE my package to accompany the pedophile, Mr. Oily Nose. After he's released from the hospital, he's taken into police custody and is currently awaiting trial. Biker Dudes against Pedophiles are being linked to the attack, though of course there is no direct evidence. Thanks to what happened with my copycat, Catalina, the Masked Savior is long gone, or rather "dead", and no one even mentions the name.

Now if I would've used my Taser and Zip Ties, that'd be a different story. Rumors of the Masked Savior would've resurfaced. Which goes to show, I need to continuously mix things up. The animal control pole had been a last minute thought and admittedly a genius one. It's a good way to control an "animal" from a safe distance. Because an animal is what a person like Mr. Oily Nose is. Yes, the pole is definitely something I'll use again.

That and a four-inch number two Phillips head Craftsman screwdriver. Tax and all, five-seventy-four. Red and yellow handle, just like the one Stabber Brother used.

I pay cash for it and smiling, I walk from the store. I'm

discovering that it's the preparation that makes me the happiest.

As I unlock my Jeep, my cell rings. It's Adam. "Nice job," he says, "wrapping up the pedophile."

"Thanks," I genuinely say, liking the fact I can share this accomplishment with someone. I close my door and fit my key in, excited to move on to the next steps—to stalking Stabber Brother, to planning, to organizing... But before I can put my phone on speaker, Adam keeps talking.

"I'm sitting down the block from the half-way house where our stabber currently resides. It would be easy to make it look like another parolee did it. That stuff happens all the time. Except with that, there'd be a lot of inquiries and bleeding hearts whining about rehabilitation. No, this needs to be done off the property. Every day he rides a bus to his job bagging groceries. He works the afternoon shift and is expected to be checked into the half-way house at nine p.m. A time, of course, that he won't be present for. The house where the stabbing occurred has long since sold, and the mom and sister have moved. The new owners are away for the week on a cruise. This is the week it should be done and his body left in the garage in the same location where he did his sister." He pauses. "Thoughts?"

Adam has more of a capacity and desire for this than I imagined. Plus, he's just taken away all of my preparatory fun.

31

THAT NIGHT I'M sitting passenger side in Adam's beat up Chevy, letting him take the lead in this. Or rather letting him think he's taking the lead. I'm trying to keep an open mind.

"See that door right there?" Adam asks, nodding through the night and across the alley to the back of the half-way house. "He comes out of the door every night at exactly ten to take out the garbage. That's when we take him."

"I thought you wanted to take him when he gets off work."

"I changed my mind. It's better if he checks in, that way they think he's on property." Adam points up to the windows. "Blinds are always closed. No one will know he's even gone until they come out to look for him."

"Hm," I agree because actually, that's not a bad idea.

I glance right to the empty and wooded lot beside the half-way house, and to the left where a tiny breakfast hut stands, closed at this time of night. Adam's right. No one will see a thing.

Pushing his glasses up, he shifts to look at me. "'Be careful what you think you know about someone.' I hear Mom say that all the time and those words have been coming back to me a lot lately."

I'm not sure if Adam is talking about me or Stabber Brother, but his mom is right. Be careful indeed. "Why risk all of this?" I decide to ask him, curious of his answer.

"Because there are too many people that get away with too many things, and if I can somehow re-balance that equation, I'm doing it. I know you understand what I'm saying."

I do, and while his reasons come across principled, my reasons include so many more layers. Like the fact, I need to do this. I crave it. It's the only way I myself maintain that balance.

Adam puts his car in gear and rolls down the alley. "Okay, so tomorrow night is the night. We'll use my car since it has a trunk. We'll hide behind the garbage…"

On and on Adam goes, detailing his plan, and idly I listen, imagining he and I doing this together. Me jumping in with both feet and seeing if this alliance calls to me. Really trying to visualize not being alone and relying on someone else. I can sort of see it, but it feels different, like uncharted territory and oddly exhilarating. Almost like we're going into business together.

But don't people say not to go into business with family or friends? Still, without Adam, Stabber Brother wouldn't even be on my radar.

In my peripheral vision, I see Adam yawn and rub one eye. It's not even nine o'clock at night. "Tired?" I ask.

He shrugs. "Haven't slept well the last couple of nights."

Hm, and here I thought he was "sleeping like a baby".

People that don't sleep well have things on their mind. Things like the fate of Stabber Brother.

Adam lets out a little chuckle. "Okay, I'll admit I'm a little nervous. I mean, aren't you?"

No, not about Stabber Brother, but definitely about Adam. I don't say this, though, and instead chuckle, too. "Yes, of course."

Truth is, what makes me think I can count on Adam? He's new to this. He doesn't know what he's getting into.

Be careful what you think you know about someone. I think about those words and what they really mean. We see two things in people—what we want to see and what they want to show us. Really, I don't know Adam any more than he knows me.

Just like Victor and my mom. A married couple. Raising three kids. Both at the FBI. Seemingly as close as a couple can be and yet an infinite distance between them.

Adam pulls up outside of my house, and Tommy's here, propped on his bike, arms and legs folded, waiting on me. I don't hide the smile the creeps into my cheeks.

Putting the car in park, Adam asks, "Who's that?"

"My boyfriend," I say, oddly content with those words and that knowledge.

"That's Tommy? Good job. He's hot."

My gaze slides to Adam, and I watch as he appreciatively takes in the long and lean deliciousness that is Tommy. "Mine," I say and Adam laughs.

"Tomorrow night," he reminds me, and with a nod, I open the door and climb out. "Thanks for this," he says through the window.

"Yep, that's what friends are for."

As Adam drives off, I stalk my way over to Tommy.

Would the neighbors care if I did him right here on his motorcycle? Yes, probably.

I don't stop as I slide my body against his and my tongue slips right into his mouth. He responds by grabbing my ass and pulling me in closer.

A few heated minutes later and with his erection pressing against me, I eye the motorcycle he's still propped against. "Ever done it on your motorcycle?"

He nibbles my neck. "No, but I'm up for the challenge."

I reach between us, grasping his erection and a throat clearing has Tommy pulling back, not me. It's a neighbor strolling the sidewalk behind us and Tommy chuckles a little as he gently pushes me away.

I'm not a pouter, but I could probably do a really good one right now if I wanted to.

Tommy holds a hand up, warning me to stay a distance away. "Actually, I came over here to ask you out on a date."

"Oh." Because I was so ready to go find an alley and do the motorcycle thing.

His lips twitch. "But should I be worried? I mean, we've only been official for a few days and you're already coming home with another guy."

I smile at his joking. "That's Adam and he thinks you're hot."

Tommy shrugs a shoulder. "Shucks."

I don't go into any more details about Adam. "So, date? What did you have in mind? And more importantly, can it begin, or end, with my motorcycle idea?"

Dropping his head, Tommy laughs. "Jesus, Lane, you're killing me."

"It does sound like it would be the highlight," I freely admit.

"What about this weekend?" he redirects me. "Ever been

zip-lining? There's a course in Maryland I've been wanting to try."

That'll be perfect. Enough time to do Stabber Brother and even some recon on the still-at-large strangler. "Sounds great."

"Good." He goes to get back on his bike. "Your dad doing okay?"

I love that he just asked me that. "Yes, better." On a quick cover-my-ass thought I say, "I heard they called you the night it happened looking for me. Sorry about that, miscommunication on my schedule."

"All good." He clips his helmet on, cranks the engine, and with a wink, rumbles off.

Yet another thing I like about Tommy—he doesn't pry or question. He gets my need for space and privacy. Just like I get his.

32

NEVER UNDERESTIMATE THE capacity of people to let you down. Never underestimate that someone you know may sell you out. Always look out for number one.

These are all the things that circle my brain in a mad loop as I sit behind the wheel of my Jeep staring at the store where Stabber Brother bags groceries. I don't know why I'm thinking those words. Adam has yet to let me down. Call it self-preservation, I guess.

Yes, those words are on repeat because way in the recess of my mind, I know Adam is waiting on me at the half-way house and I'm 99.9 percent sure I'm not going to show. Because the more I sit here, the more I want Stabber Brother all to myself.

This is Adam's vengeance, not mine, but I can't seem to help it. I tell myself I'm doing Adam a favor, not letting him fully into this darkness, but I also know I'm going to owe him even more. First I accidentally kill his brother and now I'm knowingly taking Stabber Brother from him.

I'm not exactly sure how I'm going to do this. A few

scenarios have gone through my mind. What I do know is that I have to do it before Stabber Brother reaches the half-way house. Because once he's there, he's fair game to Adam.

Unseen, unnoticed, and perfect—things I'm wishing for but am not sure I can pull off. I hate to improvise, but Adam's leaving me no choice.

Stabber Brother exits the grocery store then and stands to the side while he lights a cigarette. From the information Adam sent me, I know this guy is five-eight, twenty years old, and one-hundred-forty pounds. With his red hair, freckled skin, and green eyes, we could be brother and sister.

In the darkness of my Jeep, I watch him inhale and then exhale. I try to picture him stabbing his little sister those five years ago, and I can't seem to form the scene. I'm certain of course that he did it, and I'm certain that he's the one who has been active in the chat room and bragging about the stabbing.

Well, I say I'm certain, but I'm operating solely off of the information Adam gave me and not my own research. I'm pressed for time, though, so I work with what I have.

It's one thing to do a horrible act, like a stabbing, and to truly regret it and make amends, but it's another whole thing to do said act and then revel in it like Stabber Brother has been doing.

I keep staring at him standing there smoking a cigarette, waiting for the recognition to occur. Waiting for that deviant part of me to recognize him, but it doesn't happen. Perhaps I need to get closer.

He moves then, pushing off the brick wall he's leaning against, and I expect him to cross through the parking lot toward the bus stop that will take him back to the half-way house. But he doesn't and instead walks the length of the storefront. At this hour, only the grocery store remains open and the others—the running store, the shoe store, the pet store, and several others—have all closed for the evening.

I don't know where Stabber Brother is going. If he's going to make it back by curfew, he only has thirty minutes or so to dally.

With my window down, I put my Jeep in gear and creep through the parking lot, following him. A waft of fried chicken from the nearby Popeye's flows through on the summer breeze, and I inhale deeply. It's been a while since I had fried chicken.

Stabber Brother disappears around the corner and into the alley, and that deviant part of me I was waiting for urges me to follow. In my cargo pockets, I have multiple things stuffed—duct tape, pepper spray, pocket knife, Taser, zip ties...—not exactly sure what I'll be in the mood for. It seems variety is quickly becoming my favorite. My bokken lays strapped along my back, and the screwdriver I've secured to my calf.

Parking my Jeep, I climb out and I whisper foot it over to the alley. A slight quiver passes over my skin, and I feel exposed and unready, and I know it has everything to do with the quickness of this whole thing. If it were just me, I would spend weeks following Stabber Brother and really learning him inside and out. As it is though, I don't have a definitive plan, only a vague outline, and my spine crawls with the uncomfortableness of it.

I come up against the corner of the alley, merging with the darkness and a wave of euphoria rolls through me. I recognize the sensation and the giddiness of it makes the world feel right.

Leaning away from the wall, I peak around a dumpster to see Stabber Brother sitting on the ground cross-legged, his back to me, still smoking a cigarette. His head is bowed, and I can't see what he's doing, but from the faint glow, I think it must be a phone or a tablet, considered contraband at a half-way house.

From my pocket, I pull out my mask, but an impromptu idea has me pausing and getting a little more excited. I think the mask should be for him, not me.

I slip around the dumpster, coming up right behind him. My left arm slides around his neck, putting him into a head-lock. "Don't move and don't make a sound."

"What the—" he yanks against me. The cigarette falls into his lap and the phone clatters to the ground.

I tighten my hold, knowing exactly how much pressure puts the person on the precipice of breathing. He hisses for breath, followed by a gasp, and I simply tighten my hold. Why can't people listen? "I said, don't move and don't make a sound."

Stabber Brother falls quiet, and with my left arm still around his neck, I take the mask and slip it over his head, backward so he can't see. Duct tape comes next, and I yank both of his arms hard behind his back, ratcheting the tape around his wrists.

"If it's money you're looking for, my wallet—"

I punch him hard, my fist connecting with his eye. "I said, don't talk."

From underneath the mask, his breath shudders and something way in the depths of my soul lets out a dark chuckle.

Tape goes around his ankles next and off balance he falls to the side. I leave him there while I pick up the phone and look at the screen. The chat room is up and active, his pseudo right there front and center. "StabberBro?" I ask. "Really? You couldn't come up with anything better."

"P-please," he blubbers and I kick him hard in the ribs.

"I said don't talk." I slip one finger free of my glove and scroll his contraband phone, going to his pictures next. There are naked photos of women that he's downloaded and probably whacks off to, but there are even more photos of people who have been stabbed with various objects— glass, tools, knives.

"Planning on branching out?" I ask, but he doesn't answer. Smart guy.

Adam's right. Stabber Brother needs to be dealt with.

I slip my finger back inside my glove and wipe down the phone. "Let's talk about your sister."

"Oh, shit."

"Yeah, oh shit." Tearing off a piece of duct tape, I squat down in front of him, lift the mask enough to see his pale lips, and I smash the tape across, giving it a good cramming. "I'm going to need you quiet for what I have in mind."

He mumbles something, jerking away, and I merely stand and walk to the end of the alley. I give the dark parking lot a good once over. Other than a few cars here and there, the grocery store at the far end, and my jeep parked in the shadows at the other end, the place sits empty. No one will hear a thing.

Back down the alley, I go to where Stabber Brother still lays on his side, trussed and waiting on me. "Ideally, I would have done this in the garage where you flipped your shit on your sister, but sometimes one has to improvise."

More mumbling, or rather muffled sobbing, and instead of softening me, it hardens my resolve. I imagine his sister, laying there in the garage, helpless, sobbing for help. A whimper comes next, and I slide the screwdriver from where I'd strapped it to my lower leg.

"Four-inch number two Phillips head Craftsman screwdriver. Red and yellow handle." I stroke the length of it as I advance on him and his entire body begins violently shaking.

I roll him over, climbing on top. I lift the screwdriver, aiming for the right shoulder, and my heart leaps into a full racing pulse that makes my hand quiver. But not a quiver of fear, a quiver of anticipation.

With a sure thrust, I come down into his shoulder, just like he did he sister. Skin gives, muscle tears, blood spurts, Stabber Brother jerks with a muffled scream. A pressure rises in me, climbing for release, but nothing happens.

I flip him over, and he begins to crawl away the best he can with his duct-taped wrists and legs. Yes, he tries just like his sister did. But I'm having none of that. The screwdriver goes into his other shoulder next, the one on the left, harder than the right and meeting bone.

The pressure is there again, growing inside of me, like something extraordinary is just beyond my grasp. Again, though, it doesn't come.

In a disappointed and confused few seconds, I stare down at the blood seeping out to darken his gray tee. I wait for the confusion to lift, but it doesn't. I almost forget to breathe.

His body moves again, and reality snaps back. Two more to go. This time the screwdriver, dripping now in blood, goes into his ribs, right between the second and third with more of a give as it encounters cartilage.

I glance up at the moon, glowing happily down at me, and for an unexplained reason, everything becomes necessary and right. The sureness of those two things take hold and for a moment I just stand and stare up at the moon in the perfect star-filled night.

But again Stabber Brother moves and I come back to

myself. Last one. An unexplained shiver runs through me, making me sense something just there within reach. Something important and pure. Something so clear I should be able to hold it, but I can't.

My gaze fixates on Stabber Brother and the C-one spot. The last insertion point. The one that severed his sister's spine and put her in a lifelong paralyzed state. Anger festers in me at the injustice. The way his sister lay there, helpless and hurt, confused and desperate. The anger morphs into rage so quickly that my skin buzzes with electrical heat.

Like an animal, I want to roar. Instead, I tighten my grip on the handle, plant my boot into his mid back to keep him steady, and I come straight down. What a repulsive slug of a human being. A tingle of response tickles down my spine and through both arms and legs, like I'm on the brink of something wonderful, but not quite there yet.

His body thrashes and leaves me unsure if I hit the right spot.

As I'm contemplating whether to stop or to try again, whether to put more exploration into that teetering sense of release and satisfaction, the static sound of a guard's radio filters through the night.

I stare down at this grub of a being, knowing I'm done. We're done. The nearby guard is forcing my retreat and filling me with even more loathing. Just look at Stabber Brother, taped up, bloody, still trying to squirm away. The sight of him now seems rash and messy and leaves me with regret. Not regret I did it, just that I can do better.

Still, I give him a hard knock in the head, making sure he's out. I grab the mask and sprint from the back side of the alley, leaving Stabber Brother as is, with the screwdriver and the contraband phone. All of that coupled with who he is will speak for itself.

Woods border the back of the building and I cut through them, eventually finding my way to a neighborhood, then on foot circling the long way back around the string of stores to my Jeep parked a distance away.

The guard obviously found Stabber Brother because cops are there now on the other side of the lot, along with an ambulance, their lights spinning and strobing through the night. I should feel satisfied with what I did to Stabber Brother, but instead, I'm moody as I climb in and drive away.

Something about the whole thing feels off. None of it would have happened if it weren't for Adam. Yeah, he really came through in pointing me in Stabber Brother's direction. This was his idea so maybe that is what feels off. He should've been involved. I shouldn't have done it by myself.

He'll be disappointed, angry even. I'll explain it to him, though. I'll say I was at the grocery store, making sure Stabber Brother made it to the bus, and that I was planning to follow him to the half-way house. I'll say I saw him wander off and knew I needed to move.

Adam will be peeved and likely sense my deception, but I'll apologize and he'll forgive me.

The truth is, I'm not ready to share this experience. Yet somehow I know when I am, it'll be Adam that I share it with. He does seem to embrace who I am. Maybe then the off-ness that I feel will turn to right.

33

A SCREAM RICOCHETS through my brain, and I shoot straight out of a dead sleep into complete wakefulness. Down the hall, Victor's door opens, and I sit up in bed.

Through the dimly lit upper floor, he looks at me. "Are you okay?"

"That wasn't me," I tell him, swinging my legs over and sliding from bed.

He veers off to the right, quietly opening Justin's door, and I head left into Daisy's room. Under her pale green comforter and through the shadows, I see her body moving and squirming. She mumbles something, groaning, and I make my way over her throw rug to the double bed.

"Daisy," I whisper, giving her shoulder a little shake.

More grumbling, followed by a whimper. What the hell?

"Daisy," I say louder, more firmly shaking her shoulder.

"What?" she gasps.

I try to make out her face, but she doesn't sleep with a night light like the rest of us. "Are you okay?"

Breathing out, she pushes the comforter down and sits up. "God, I'm covered in sweat."

"Everything okay in here?" Victor asks, and I give him a little wave. "Okay, I'll leave my door open if you two need anything."

I lower myself onto the edge of her bed, my eyes better adjusting to her dark room. "Want to tell me about it?"

She scrubs her hands over her face. "That was crazy."

"What did you dream?"

"I don't think I want to tell you."

I want to turn a light on but decide to keep it dark. It's easier to share secrets in the dark. "You know you can tell me anything. No matter how weird or strange or off it is. Okay? I will never judge." I've told her this before, but she needs to hear it again.

She glances over her shoulder at the open door, and I take that as my cue to go close it. When I'm back on her bed, I grab her mug of herbal tea that she sips ever night as she's reading. There's a little bit left in it and she eagerly drinks it down.

With the mug gripped tightly, she begins in a quiet voice, "I was in a room, and the walls were covered with shelves that held glass containers with body parts. Organs and fingers and toes. Eyeballs and ears and feet. It looked like some were human and some were animals. I was in the center of the room carving up a brain. I was humming to myself. Then Mom walked in, carrying one of those containers and slid it onto the shelf along with the others. She came over to where I was standing and looked over my shoulder, smiling. Then you walked in, carrying a dog. I think it was that Corn Chip you always play with. He was happy and licking your face. Then you put him on the table and he began eating the brain." Daisy shakes her head. "What the hell, Lane?"

It isn't until she stops speaking that I realize I'm not even breathing, so I inhale a breath that comes in almost like a gasp. For a second there I thought she was going to say I killed Corn Chip. "Is that all?"

"Isn't that enough?"

Logic tells me that something similar to this may have happened. Her dream was likely a mixture of fantasy and reality. I mean, Aunt Marji had me dismembering a cat when I was just a toddler. Thankfully, I only know this through the letters I found. I don't want that memory to surface. But this room she dreamt about could have been anywhere. For all I know it may have been at that trailer where I tracked Aunt Marji. Where I then killed her.

The need to tell Daisy everything rises up, but this isn't the right time. I know that. "Listen, I've had a lot of weird dreams, too, since Mom died."

"Weird like I just had?"

Of course I haven't, but still, I say, "Yes, absolutely. A serial killer butchered our mom. Dr. Issa was stabbed to death. It's not like we've had an easy year. Our minds are odd things and they take things you read, things you watch, things you hear, and twists and mangles it into a mutilated version. I'm sorry you had that nightmare, but that's all it was, a nightmare. Nothing about it was real. It's your body's way of responding to anxiety and stress."

Daisy chuckles. "Maybe I need to start reading fairy tales before I go to bed."

"I don't know. Fairy tales can be creepy. Maybe read a trashy magazine. Then you'll dream you're a housewife of Beverly Hills."

"Ha!"

With a smile, I take her mug and put it back on the bedside table.

Daisy crawls out of bed. "Thanks, Lane, I'm glad we have each other." She pads out of her room and into the bathroom, but I don't immediately move.

This isn't good. That dream unsettles me.

34

THAT AFTERNOON I decide to go find Adam before he finds me. With what happened in the alley with Stabber Brother, I ignored Adam's texts that came in afterward and went straight home. With the event being on the news this morning, I know he knows what I did.

It's time I see how this is going to play out.

I find Adam in the side yard of his McMansion, throwing a ball with his new puppy. He hears my Jeep and glances over his shoulder, and even from here I see the anger on his pale face.

I ignore it though as I climb out and cross his decorative brick driveway over onto the grass. "You alone?"

"Yep." He grabs the tennis ball and gives it a good hard throw and the puppy yips his way across the grass.

"Did you name her yet?"

"Nope."

"You seem angry."

"I am."

"Maybe you need to blow off some steam."

"Maybe you need to shut the hell up."

O-kay. I don't let people talk to me this way, but I owe this boy, so I channel tolerance with his mood. I want to launch right into my reasons for doing Stabber Brother alone, to my reasons for ditching Adam, but something tells me I need to keep quiet.

The puppy comes yapping back toward us, carrying the ball, and Adam doesn't bother praising the puppy, squatting to rub it, or giving the ball another toss. He's too caught up in his own annoyance and frustration with me.

Leaning down, I do exactly what you're supposed to. I praise the puppy, rubbing behind her dark furry ears, and then I tug-of-war a few seconds with the tennis ball before slinging it back down the yard.

Adam turns to me. "There's a lot of wrong in this world, Lane, and that was my friend we were getting justice for. It was supposed to be you and me and the brother. Not you and him. Hell, it should have been me and the brother, and not you. What don't you get about that?"

I remind myself I killed his older brother, Scott, and I did purposefully do the alley screwdriver stabbing without him. I will be patient. "Listen, it really was an accident. He didn't go to his bus like we thought. He headed in a different direction. I knew if I didn't do something, the opportunity would pass."

"Then we could have done it another night like planned."

I hold my hands up, proud of myself for keeping my calm. "I'm sorry."

With a sigh, Adam drags his gaze away from mine and down to where the puppy is now rolling around in the grass. "Maybe I'll find someone else then."

My brows go up. "Come again?"

Adam shrugs. "He was just a symptom to a screwed-up system. I've been doing a little digging, and really it's the prison counselor's fault who let him go early. Turns out that counselor has a record for just this thing—signing off on good behavior and convincing the parole board the prisoner is ready for society. Yeah, it's the prison counselor who is the root to these type problems. Freakin' bloodsucking, soulless person."

Adam has officially lost it. He can't go and "off" the counselor who recommended Stabber Brother be released. I try for reason, "Listen, with that mindset then you need to trace it back to the lawyer and the judge and the arresting officer... Everyone is just doing their job, surely you see that."

"You're right, it's not just about the counselor, it is about everyone else. They're warping and twisting the system. They're putting people on the streets that don't deserve to be."

I don't want my mind to draw comparisons, but this is ringing way too close to my experience with my copycat, Catalina. She targeted all these innocent people who didn't deserve it. So far, Adam has been nothing like Catalina, and I understand he's angry and going off on the system. I also understand I am the catalyst for this anger. If I would have let him help me with Stabber Brother, he would feel avenged right now, not all wound up.

Or would he? It's hard to tell. Maybe this is exactly how he would be no matter how Stabber Brother went down. Either way, I can't knock the feeling that I'm responsible for Adam. This is my fault.

I try for reason one more time with someone I know he cares about. "What about your uncle, Judge Penn? Think about all those people he's been forced to let go because the law won't allow him to sentence them. With your train of thought, he would fall into your hit list, too. You and I both know your uncle would put every single one of those people away if given the chance. He's one of the good ones."

With a sigh, Adam closes his eyes, and he shakes his head. He doesn't say anything, and I hope my words are really sinking in and showing him reason. I don't say anything. I just watch and observe and wait for the truth of what I said to sink fully in.

The puppy comes barreling back toward us, panting, the ball happily lodged between her teeth. I start to lean down to praise her, and Adam beats me to it, giving her a good rub down, and pointing her to the water bowl.

Okay, I think Adam's back.

Still squatted down, he looks up at me, and I see a friendlier version of the Adam he was showing me seconds ago. I see the Adam I've come to know. "You're right, and I'm sorry. Can we forget what I just said? I don't know what I was thinking."

I nod, and in the interest of friendship, say, "It's forgotten. And Adam, I really am sorry I did the brother without you. I honestly didn't plan it, it just happened." That much is true. I didn't go there with intent, I slowly developed it.

He gives a slight nod, and I study his light brown eyes, looking for the understanding. Honestly, I can't read him, but my gut tells me he's not sure if he believes me.

Smart boy.

I really want to nudge him again on The Strangler but again now is not the right time.

35

T HAT NIGHT AS I'm going to bed, Adam begins
texting me.

Adam: DO YOU EVER THINK ABOUT THE
OTHER SIDE?

Me: OTHER SIDE?

Adam: When someone dies, and they go away. Is it
heaven or hell or someplace else?

Me: I don't know.

Honestly, I don't think about that stuff.

Adam: What about ending someone's life? Would you
do it if it meant they were out of pain?

Me: You mean like a terminal patient?

Adam: Yeah.

Me: Yes, I would.

Adam: But it's illegal and a sin.

Me: So is a bunch of stuff.

Adam: Good point.

I stare at my phone, trying to figure out where he's going
with this, but a lot of minutes go by and nothing else comes

in. All I can think is, who the hell is he thinking about killing?

Adam: SIGNING OFF. GOODNIGHT.

Me: 'NIGHT.

It takes me a little more time than usual to fall asleep, and the restlessness reminds me of the months following my mom's death. I couldn't seem to get my brain and body leveled out, and as I think through the dreams and nightmares that I had during that time, I begin to drift off...

Adam looks up at me from his hospital bed. "I know your secret, Lane."

I look around the room. "Why are you in here?"

"If you help me die, you think you'll be like her. Your mother."

I shake my head. "I don't know what you're talking about."

"The Decapitator."

"That wasn't my mother."

"I did some digging on you. I put it all together." Adam reaches out and takes my hand. "It's okay, Lane. You'll never be like her."

My eyes open, and I stare at the shadows playing across the ceiling of my bedroom. Restlessness, dreams, it means my mind isn't at repose which is completely understandable given my new friendship with Adam.

There is no way he knows my mother was the Decapitator.

This is my first thought, and it's immediately followed by another one that has me sitting straight up in bed.

Is Adam dying?

36

THE NEXT NIGHT Victor has the D.A. and Adam over for dinner. I like that Victor's reaching out to the family. I like that my stepdad and the D.A. used to be high school friends and are becoming that again. He needs friends, and I like the D.A., especially now that I know her and Judge Penn are related, because I've always liked Penn. I like Adam, too, even though our friendship can be weird.

Seems like I like a lot right now.

There's just something so normal about having dinner. Sitting around the table. Talking. Laughing. The smell of pot roast. Tearing off a chunk of bread. Washing dishes. Yes, it's all so normal. So mundane, I guess, and soothing. Maybe this is what life is supposed to feel like.

"Show me your room?" Adam asks after dinner.

The only reason he's asking that is because he wants to talk. I'm not entirely sure what he wants to bring up, but I'm curious enough to see. Maybe he wants to tell me he's dying. I don't like thinking that.

When we get to my room, Adam closes my door, giving

us privacy. I knew it. He doesn't want to "see my room", he wants to talk. I brace myself. If he wants me to help him commit suicide, I honestly do not know how I'm going to respond. Is he really that sick? He doesn't look sick.

From the front pocket of his shorts, he pulls out a flash drive. "Everything I could find on the strangled girls."

I wasn't expecting this and am relieved this isn't about possible assisted suicide. Excitedly I reach out to take it, but he doesn't give it to me. I should tell him a keep-away-from-Lane game is not one he wants to play.

"First," he says, "have you given any more thought to our previous discussion?"

Shit. "Last night's texting? What about it?"

He shakes his head, looking confused. "No, about the prison counselor."

It's not often I'm caught off guard, but I am right now. I thought we put that topic to rest. "Adam, I still feel the same way. You, *we*, can't go after an innocent person." I nod to the flash drive he's still holding. "The Strangler is the type of person who deserves our focus."

"I see." Adam puts the flash drive back into his pocket, and I narrow my eyes. He is definitely pushing the line with me. "I thought we were friends."

"We are."

"Well, if you were my friend, you would help me."

I wonder if this is what Reggie felt like when she said no to me. If so, I get it.

I lean in. "Help you what, exactly? Are you actually asking me to help you take out a prison counselor? A man who has done nothing wrong except facilitate the release of a few people who shouldn't have been placed back into society." I tap my forehead. "Don't you realize how insane that sounds?"

Adam narrows his own eyes. "So what you're saying is that you're not going to help me?"

Leaning back, I fold my arms. "With the prison counselor? No."

This time, Adam leans in. "Well, then, fuck you."

Conflict resolution is not my strong point, and he is officially over the line now. "(A) I hate that word and (B) you need to go."

37

MY CONVERSATION WITH Adam has me thinking about Reggie pretty much nonstop the rest of the night. Dialing her number is the first thing I do in the morning. I'm surprised that I find myself nervous as I wait for the call to go through.

It's been months since we talked.

Reggie and I met years ago at a Science and Technology summer camp. We immediately did and have always gotten each other. Reggie's one of those friends you can hang out with and never say a word. She's one of those friends you're automatically comfortable with.

She goes to MIT and we used to talk or text daily. I screwed that up, though. I asked too much of her friendship. I took her for granted. I let my own desires get in the way of the truthfulness that has always been she and I.

"Yo," she answers, just like she has a million times before. Like no time has passed. Like she doesn't wonder why I'm calling.

I don't take the friendly greeting for granted and launch right in, saying, "Reggie, I'm so sorry for being a bad friend.

And I'm even sorrier for taking you for granted. Will you forgive me?"

"Let's FaceTime," she says and clicks over before I have a chance to answer her.

Her familiar pretty face fills my screen, and I smile. "Hi," I say.

She smiles back, and the dimple in her right cheek sinks in. "You cut your hair."

"Yeah." I look at her shaved head. She's shaved it before and has the face to pull it off, but the last time I saw her it was longer. "So did you."

Reggie makes a face. "I didn't mean to this time. I tried to color it purple and the process fried my hair. Shaving it was the only way to make it healthy again."

"Well, like I said the last time you did it, you've got the face for it."

"Thanks. Hey, how's Daisy and Justin and your dad? Everyone holding up okay?"

Reggie came for Mom's funeral and checked in with me nearly every day after that. Reggie loved my mom. "Everyone's really good. Daisy and I are remarkably friends. Justin is having fun at summer camp. Dad has recently connected with an old high school friend." I don't tell Reggie that he was in the hospital. That will only worry her.

Her dark eyes brighten. "You mean like an old high school girlfriend?"

I laugh. "A little, I think."

"I'm glad you and Daisy are getting along."

"Me, too. What about you?"

She shifts a little to lay back on her dorm bed. "Well, obviously I'm in summer school." She crinkles her nose. "I didn't want to go home."

I don't blame her. Her dad is a horrible man. "You could've come here," I tell her.

She shrugs. "It's all good. Plus with all the smarties around here, I have to do summer school just to keep up."

Reggie's being modest. She's the smartest person I know. But I don't like that she's not taking a break. "No going out then?"

"Not really."

I shift, too, propping my feet up on my desk. "I've got a boyfriend."

Reggie sits straight up. "Shut up. Are you serious?"

I laugh again. "Yes, his name's Tommy. He's tall and blonde and rides a motorcycle."

"Oh my God, please send me a pic." She lowers her voice. "Have you done the nasty yet?"

"We've done oral, but no penetration."

Reggie gags. "I hate the word penetration."

On our conversation goes, from Tommy back to school. From her study partner to my new college plans. From her asshole dad to my new friend, Adam. We talk for nearly thirty more minutes before I cycle the conversation back around.

"Reggie, I really am sorry I screwed things up between us. You're my best friend. I've missed this. Will you forgive me?"

She smiles. "I already have."

38

DOWNSTAIRS, VICTOR IS packing Justin a lunch for his camp field trip into D.C. "You're down kind of late."

"I was talking to Reggie."

"Did you guys make up?"

I grab a mug and pour coffee. "Yes, but now I'm fighting with Adam—" I stop myself. When did I become so share-y?

Victor puts a string cheese into the paper bag and folds it over. "Well, friends fight."

"I'm not sure Adam would call me a friend right now."

With a sharpie, Victor writes Justin's name on the bag. "You're a great friend, Lane. Never doubt that."

Am I really? I don't know. I'd like to think I am to the right people. Or if I veer off course, I'd like to think I recognize my mistakes and correct my direction. A year ago I would say the problem was Adam, but now I don't. Maybe that comes with maturity.

Either way, life was fine before him and it'll certainly go on.

Grabbing the remote, I flip on the T.V. and the headline is all about a new strangled girl. That makes four in all now. Forget about Adam, I'm figuring this out on my own.

39

LATER THAT MORNING I pull up a map of the area. The only information I have is that the girls are all young and they all have dark hair. I also know where the strangled bodies were found and their names. This is all public information.

Caley, Zabrina, Evelyn, and Yasmin. I write down each of the girl's names and everything I can find on them: family, friends, activities, school. The one thing I immediately note is that they all live in Loudoun County, just like Ted Lowman and Scott Butler. They do not all go to the same school though and range in age from sixteen to nineteen.

The first girl was done when Teddy was still alive and the other three were done after. The first girl is the whole reason why Teddy hit my radar and I began to watch him. He either did the first girl and someone did the other three, or Teddy is completely innocent of murder and guilty only of sex with a minor, or rather multiple minors.

Next, I print off a map and put an X where each body was found. I also put a star on Ted Lowman's house, noting all the bodies were found within a five-mile radius of his home. That's almost too perfect. I also put a star on Scott Butler's apartment, but it is miles removed from any of the bodies or Ted's house.

The first body was found right over the border in Fairfax County, which explains how this landed in Penn's court. How I first stumbled across Ted Lowman.

I study all the girls and what information I have, looking for a pattern there, too. Did they know each other? Did they know Scott and/or Teddy?

I write sex tapes and put a question mark. I try to remember the names of the girls on the DVD's, but there were so many, I don't immediately recall them. I kept copies, though, after I sent the D.A. the originals. It would be a simple matter of going through them to see if any of the strangled girls make an appearance. I'm not going to do that right now, though, I'll do that later. Right now, I want to keep brainstorming.

Scarf. I write that word down. Adam had mentioned a scarf, and though that detail doesn't show up in my research, I still jot it down. From what I can remember of the sex tapes, there were no scarves used. In fact, nothing but two bodies and sex.

Scott Butler and Ted Lowman... Why was Scott over at Ted's house that night? How do they know each other? If the girls are on the sex tapes, has someone else seen them? Is that how they were picked?

Okay, backtracking to Scott and Ted. Let me see all the ways they're connected.

I do some quick searches. Ted is older than Scott by a few years, so I know they didn't go to college together. Scott was a high school guidance counselor and Ted, from what I can tell, lived off his inheritance.

Where would these two men have met?

I type in the school where Scott worked as a Guidance Counselor and find their Facebook page. I scroll through it, studying each picture.

I find one a couple years old with both Scott and Ted and a bunch of high school kids. The caption reads, "After School Program: Studying for the SAT's." I scroll through the comments and it looks like the students who attend are from all over Loudoun County, not just Scott's high school.

Okay, that makes sense.

So Ted was a tutor? Huh, I wouldn't have guessed. He didn't seem bright enough to be a tutor. But at least now I have a good idea of how Scott and Ted met. How they began their sex tape friendship.

I zoom in on several photos of this study group and scrutinize the faces. A couple of the pictures are years old, but I do find one of the strangled girls with her arm slung over a friend, grinning.

The alarm on my phone dings, telling me it's time to leave for my Patch and Paw shift. Tonight I'll browse the sex tapes and see if the strangled girls make an appearance.

40

THAT NIGHT AFTER my shift at Patch and Paw, I'm walking across the parking lot to my Jeep, and I spy Adam parked right beside me, sitting on his hood.

I don't nod an acknowledgment or say hello, I simply walk straight up to him and stand with my arms folded in front of him. The parking lot light towering behind and to the right casts an odd shadowy glow over the features of his pale face and makes his eye sockets appear deep set.

With a sigh, he pushes his glasses up. "I'm an idiot."

"Yes," I agree. "You are."

Adam lowers his head and fidgets with the key ring loosely gripped in his fingers. "I don't know what I was thinking."

"You were looking for answers. For justice."

"Yes." He lifts his head. "But not that way."

"I agree, not that way. Never by targeting someone innocent."

"Thank you for telling me no. Thank you for being a good friend."

"You're welcome."

He doesn't say anything after that, and carefully I watch him. Some long seconds stretch between us, and then he sighs. "Sometimes I feel...out of control." His gaze lifts to mine. "That sounds weird, doesn't it?"

"No," I assure him, "it doesn't."

"My mind gets bogged down by personal crap and when that happens I don't make the best decisions. Thanks for reigning me in."

I decide to use Victor's words. "Sometimes friends fight. We had a fight. Okay? All over now."

He gives me a very slight, grateful smile. "I really am sorry."

I don't do hugs, so I simply nod. "Forgiven."

Friends. Not friends. I seem to go back and forth in that area. Zach, Reggie, Tommy, Dr. Issa, and now Adam. I'd like to think I'm a good friend. Or have the potential to be a good friend. I would definitely have any one of their backs if need be. And Adam's right, real friends say no when it's not right. I said no.

"Adam, are you dying?"

He leans back. "What? No. Why would you think... Oh." Behind his glasses, he takes a second to rub his already bloodshot eyes. Patiently, I wait.

"I told you my dad died last year?" he reminds me.

"Of alcohol poisoning," I confirm.

He scoots off the hood of his car and paces away, then he turns back. "Not exactly. I, um, I ended his life."

It's not often my eyes go wide in surprise, in fact I can't recall a time they ever have, but they do now. "Okay." I wait for the rest.

Adam takes a second to zip up his lightweight hoody, and I can tell he's buying himself some thinking time. "He'd been moved to hospice, was going to die anyway. He was barely breathing, Lane, and every breath he did take went in and out in this painful whine." He paces away again. "I really hated him, and I remember thinking, 'You deserve every one of those painful breaths.' What kind of person thinks that way?"

"A normal one," I assure him.

Adam's pacing has now put him completely in the dark and out of the light streaming down from the nearby lamp. I want him to step back into the light. I want to see his face.

"He asked me to, no *begged* me to. He said it would be a gift. It would give him peace. I didn't want to give him a gift. I didn't want to give him peace. He assured me I'd be doing a good thing. But if it was so good, then why didn't I feel good about it, ya know?" He paces further into the darkness, like being not seen gives him anonymity to keep going.

"It was seeing my mom and my brother so distraught that made me do it. I wanted them to have the peace and the gift, not him. Not Dad. So I did it. I smothered him with a pillow. He didn't even struggle. I cried the whole time. I didn't think about it then, but now I constantly wonder if he asked Scott, too. Or did he know I would be the son to embrace the idea? I killed him, Lane. I ended his life."

"It's good that you did," I'm quick to reassure him. "It was mercy."

Adam moves back into the light. "Was it? Was it really?"

"Yes, for your whole family." I step into the light with him, and I put my hand on his shoulder. "You need to let it go now." I squeeze his shoulder. "Do you hear me? Let it go. It's okay. You've told me. No one else needs to know."

Adam's bottom lip quivers, and he presses them together to keep himself strong and brave. "Thank you," he murmurs, trying not to cry. "I really needed to hear that."

I said I wasn't a hugger, but I pull him in and give him one. A few seconds later and with a sniff, he pulls away. "I need to go," he says, and I nod.

As he's opening his car door, he says, "Lane?"

I glance over, and he tosses me a flash drive. He doesn't say a word, but I know it contains all the information on The Strangler.

41

"WHAT DID IT *feel like to end your mom's life?"*
Adam asks me.

"It felt like justice."

Adam nods his understanding. "We're like-minded, you and me. Imagine the great we could do in this world."

"Yeah," Catalina agrees. "Imagine."

My eyelids open, and I look at the ceiling in my bedroom and the shadows flicking eerily across it from the tree outside blowing slightly in the breeze.

That's two times now I've had a dream about Adam, but what the hell is it with my copycat, Catalina, making an appearance? Adam and Catalina are nothing alike. Yeah, initially I thought Catalina and I had made a friend connection, but that whole thing turned sour fast.

Adam's different. He's not purposefully deceiving people. He's lost and trying desperately to make sense of his life. I get that. I do.

He wanted Stabber Brother all to himself, and I took that from him. Maybe I should give it back. Maybe I should take him in, really take him in, and guide him. I've already alluded to working together on The Strangler case, but now I could really follow through with it. We could work together, truly work together. It would be nice to have someone to bounce ideas off of, someone who could back me up and vice versa. And if I feel he's ready, and in a true act of selflessness, I could give him the final act of justice.

The idea circles around inside of me, warming me. But just as quickly as I begin to feel excitement over the prospect, I think about my real parents, the Decapitator team, and the unsettling realization that I now see the appeal of a partner. Someone to share the darkness with. Someone to watch me. Someone who I can watch.

Someone who I can watch...I think about that for a second and backtrack to that alley with Stabber Brother. What would it have felt like to watch Adam do what I did? To not participate, but just to watch.

Hm, it's an interesting thought. It would take our friendship to a whole new level, that's for sure. Though it also seems like it would be the end of my perfectly constructed life. Relationships are complicated, that's for sure. Bringing Adam into my world in a real way would be a gamble, and most gamblers eventually lose.

Something to consider.

The flash drive Adam gave me is sitting on my desk, unused. The old Lane would have stayed up until three in the morning, devouring every single thing on there. I think, though, that I already knew that drive is meant to be reviewed with Adam. Even though he's already seen it, my first time reviewing it should be with him.

I want to keep thinking through things, but the need for sleep begins tugging at me. I try to blink and stay awake, but my eyes eventually stick shut on a last thought. Yes, I'll review it with Adam. I owe him that.

42

LATE THAT AFTERNOON, I drive over to Adam's house with a decision made. Like last time, he's in the side yard playing with the puppy. I love that.

I park my Jeep and climb out. As I make my way over to them, I notice that he's bought and installed a dog house, complete with climate control, windows on all sides, a porch, and steps up to a balcony. I doubt my first apartment will look better than this dog house.

"Wow," I say, coming to stand beside him. "That's a masterpiece."

Adam smiles. "It came earlier today." He motions around the gigantic yard. "Tomorrow the invisible fence goes in."

"Did you name her?"

"Sally."

I love it when people give their pets a human name. She yip-yaps her way toward me, and I squat down to love on her. She's grown quite a bit since Adam got her. I was right, Sally's going to be huge.

We spend a few sunny and breezy minutes playing with

Sally before Adam turns to me, "You stopping by to say hi or is there something else?"

From my front jean pocket, I slide out the flash drive and am surprised that I do not feel awkward or hesitant when I say, "Was thinking we might want to go through this together. Do a little brainstorming."

Adam laughs. "I've already been going through it and was going to ask you the same thing. I was hesitant though. I wasn't sure where we stood."

"Two brains are better than one and all that."

Adam glances toward his house. "Now?"

"Sure, let me just get something from the Jeep."

A few minutes later I meet him inside carrying one of my journals and the independent research I already did.

We head upstairs and into his room. It's the first time I've been up the stairs in their mansion. Everything gleams— from the wood floors to the gold doorknobs and from the ornately framed photos to the polished antique furniture. I'm sure they have someone whose job it is to keep every-thing shining.

Adam leads me through an open door and into a bedroom bigger than mine and Daisy's put together and complete with a king size bed, a lounging area, a television center, an en suite bathroom, an office, and even a mini-fridge.

I mean, really? What teenage boy needs all of this?

He crosses the recently vacuumed carpet and plops down at an L shaped desk. I take a seat in the leather swivel chair sitting off to the right. While he boots up his massive computer system, I open up my journal.

Adam gives it a side eye. "Old school, huh?"

"I don't like to leave trails." I nod to his corporate sized computer set up. "I'm leery of the cloud."

He gives my journal a pointed look. "May I?"

Not many people have seen my journals, and those that have were very much by accident. I've never voluntarily shared them with anyone. But I told myself I was going to try something new with Adam, so I force myself to hand over my most recent purchase.

This particular journal contains only those things since meeting Adam. It contains details about Scott and Ted, Mr. Oily Nose Pedophile, research on Stabber Brother, and my most recent entries regarding The Strangler.

Silently, Adam flips through the pages, carefully studying my entries and I find myself holding my breath, waiting for something, though I'm not quite sure what. His questions perhaps. Or maybe his surprise at my detailed entries and my analytical thoughts.

He glances up at me. "Something tells me this isn't the first journal you've done." He grazes over Ted's pages. "You watched. You learned his routine. Where he went and when. What he did when he got there. You were trailing him before I ever entered the picture."

I don't answer, but my silence says it all. I'm not sure how much I should tell him.

Adam taps an entry I made. "You actually met him, didn't you?"

"I thought he was The Strangler."

Adam hands me back the journal. "Where did you learn how to do all of this?"

I shrug, playing it off. "Common sense, plus both of my parents are in the FBI. I've learned a lot from them by just observing."

Turning to his computer, he types in a password that I note for later if need be. "So you're just naturally curious?"

Again, I shrug. "Like I said, both parents in the FBI make it part of my life. So, yes, curious."

A few clicks and he brings up a file. "So you would be doing this even if you hadn't met me?"

"Yes."

"Cool."

And that's all we say before we get down to business. I feel like there's so much to teach Adam. I don't want to overwhelm him. Or me. If I was going to stop this, if I was going to back out, I'm afraid it is past time. Adam and me, we're officially in this together.

Thirty minutes later we've got things sketched out on a whiteboard that Adam pulled from storage. We've got a map of the area, much like what I printed off, with red dots on each spot where the girls were found.

"Don't you think it's odd each girl is precisely placed around Ted's house?" I ask.

Adam turns away from studying the whiteboard. "The Strangler is trying to pin it on Ted. No one knows he's dead but you and me. And by the way, it's working."

"What do you mean?"

"I overhear things when Mom is on the phone. Ted Lowman is the number one suspect in The Strangler case."

"What's your mom's response to that, given the sex tape connection he has with Scott?"

Adam shakes his head. "She's so scared Scott's extracurricular activities are going to come to light. Though she's not tampering with the investigation, she's also not hard handling it like usual. I don't think she knows what she's going to do."

I try not to make promises because who the hell knows if I can keep them, but I say, "Listen, we're going to find The Strangler and after we deal with him, we're going to make sure everyone knows who he is. Ted Lowman will officially fall off the radar. Okay?" No one will know Adam stabbed him, and no one will know about the sex tapes.

Adam nods. "Okay."

We go back to work. We've got pictures of each girl, their data, and information on them dating back ten years. Hell, we even know when this one girl started her period. The internet is ridiculously full of information.

We've got close up pictures of their strangled throats, and the forensic report (thanks to Adam) details that the first girl was strangled with hands and the other three with a silk scarf.

What we have, of course, that the detectives don't is the Scott and Ted sex tape link, which brings me to that. As I had surmised, all four strangled girls are on the various videos. Let's just say sex tapes don't always give the best angles. So Adam ran facial recognition software as definitive proof.

I put the cap back on the dry erase marker. "Okay, so all the girls lived in Loudoun County and all are featured on the sex tapes. Scott and Ted either shared the videos with someone or someone hacked their system and downloaded them or—"

"Or they uploaded them to a porn site." Adam reaches under his glasses and rubs his eyes. "I can't believe my brother was involved in all of this."

I can. Family sucks. I haven't gotten around to it yet, so I tell Adam, "I'm not for sure, but I think Scott and Ted met at your brother's school. Ted was an SAT tutor. I found a picture on the school's Facebook page. If that's where they met, it could be where The Strangler comes in."

"What about all the girls from the videos? Were they in this SAT thing?"

I shrug. "I haven't gotten that far. I did see one of the strangled girls, but I haven't had time to look for the rest."

Adam immediately dives back on his computer, spending the next thirty minutes comparing the girls from the sex videos with pictures of the SAT study group. Some match and some don't. But what Adam does find is the reoccurrence of two other adults. One male and one female.

"Let's focus on the male," Adam says.

"No, both. Just because she's a female doesn't mean she's innocent." I know this all too well.

While he zooms in on their faces and begins identification, I turn back to the whiteboard and run my finger down the forensic report again. While the strangled girls had recently had sex, there was no evidence of sexual assault. They participated willingly, and though there was bruising on their wrists and ankles from being bound, the bruising pattern indicates seconds of struggle versus minutes or hours. The hypothesis being they struggled only during the last few seconds of life, not the entire time.

So it seems they knew they were being strangled and they were okay with it until they realized it was going too far.

My eyes go back to the picture of the first girl. It's one her parents provided. She's sitting on a horse, smiling, her long dark hair blowing in the breeze. "I think the first girl was a mistake, and once The Strangler got a taste of the euphoria, he fine-tuned his method to incorporate a silk scarf. There has to be significance to that scarf."

Yes, once our strangler got a taste of the darkness, he (or she) began to branch out. It's what my parents did. It's what a lot of serial killers do. They fine-tune their methods.

I think about Ted Lowman and how he ended up in Penn's court. The first girl had been at his house hours before and several people said they disappeared into his room. He claimed they were hanging out listening to music, but his DNA was found all over her clothes, which really just means she was in his house. But the strangulation pattern on her throat didn't match the size of his hands and so Ted Lowman got off.

At which point I started following him because something just didn't sit right with me about the whole thing.

"Okay, I've got I.D. on the unknown man and woman," Adam says. "According to this they're married, no kids, the woman is a nurse, and the man an engineer." Adam glances up at me. "A husband and wife killing team?"

"It happens."

43

ADAM CASTS A nervous look around the dark parking lot and the condominium community we're currently parked in. Straight ahead sits the side door that opens into the three-story building. The nurse and the engineer live on the third floor in unit 5. Mr. and Mrs. Garner.

Or as I like to refer to them, Mr. and Mrs. Strangler.

"Are you sure we want to do this?" Adam hesitantly asks. "Breaking and entering. What if we get caught?"

My eyes slide over to his. "Really, Adam? All the things we've done and now you're worried?"

He lets out a nervous laugh. "Right. You're right."

"We need to see inside. Just like we did at your brother's place. Just like I did at the pedophile's apartment. You don't really know a person until you start digging through their stuff." I take in his anxious expression. Maybe I made a mistake bringing him here.

"No, no, I'm ready," he assures me like he can read my mind, and starts to pull his gloves on.

I stop him. "Not now. Wait. It's summer out and warm. We'd look weird walking in wearing gloves."

"Yeah, yeah, you're right." Adam sits straight up in my Jeep, nodding to the side door. "There they are," he whispers.

As expected, Mr. and Mrs. Strangler emerge from the building, her in scrubs and him in a suit. They kiss goodbye and head to separate cars. She's working the night shift, and he's heading to a business dinner. We know this because Adam hacked their wifi and their personal accounts.

"They look so normal," Adam says.

Don't they all? He's twenty-seven and she's twenty-eight. Married five years. Met at the hospital where she works. He's five-ten and she's five-eight. Both are runners. Both have brown hair. To anyone, they are "normal".

We'll see about that.

Their cars clear the parking lot, and I open my door. "Let's go."

We walk straight toward the building's side door and Adam swipes a card security key he created by hacking the building's system. Yeah, this partner thing might be a good idea.

The stairwell sits directly to the right and we trot up the steps to the third floor. The door opens to a long carpeted hallway, making the building seem more like a hotel than a place where people actually live.

We pass unit 1, 2, 3...and come to stop at the white door for unit 5.

"You seem so calm," Adam whispers.

Yeah, I probably should seem more nervous. My calmness is a giant red flag that I'm way too acquainted with this lifestyle. "Beta-blocker," I tell him.

"Oh, that's a good idea."

I slip my gloves on, and he does the same. I punch in the code to their door (again, thanks to Adam) and with a slight beep, it opens into a living room. My core temperature runs hot, and I welcome the frigid air they have the unit set to. Thank you, Mr. and Mrs. Strangler.

The place looks recently cleaned with polished tile floors, pale green fabric couches, and gleaming wood furniture. A salt lamp sits over in the corner, providing the only light. The master suite spans the area to the left and on the other side of the living room sits an open kitchen. One bedroom, clean, and organized condominium—it'll be easy to search.

Adam shuffles in. "So what are we looking for?"

"Anything. Proof that our suspicions are correct."

Adam heads into their bedroom, and I go straight to their kitchen. I spend a few seconds looking in the cookie jar and in the coffee canister. I open up a cereal box and rifle through their vitamin collection. Nothing weird here.

The living room comes next but there's nothing to search. There is no entertainment center, just a big screen attached to the wall. My gaze goes across the black and white photos framed and hanging on the pale blue walls.

I wander into their bedroom and find Adam in their walk-in closet with Mrs. Strangler's things on the right and Mr. Strangler's things on the left. Color coordinated, perfectly spaced hangers, shoes neatly on display.

"I'm afraid to touch anything," Adam says. "It's too organized. They'll know."

"I agree."

Back in their bedroom, an office takes up one corner and I head over to browse their filing cabinet. It's not even locked and I carefully thumb through the alphabetized and labeled folders. INSURANCE, MORTGAGE, KIA...

Nothing here either and I turn to see Adam sliding open the drawers of their matching maple dressers.

Another flat screen sits mounted on their wall with an internal DVD player. I push the eject button and find the slot empty.

I think we've wasted our time.

As Adam closes one drawer and opens the next, my eyes fall to the king size bed, the maroon comforter, and the dust ruffle. Who has a dust ruffle?

Kneeling down on the white throw rug, I peek under their bed and see a large brown leather trunk with black hinges. I try not to get too excited as I slide it out into the open and find it locked.

Using my picks, I work the lock and a few seconds later it pops open. I don't bother hiding my smirk. Gotcha.

Moving in to look over my shoulder, Adam lets out a low whistle. "Yes."

I run my gloved fingers over the items: restraint kit, handcuffs, whip, blindfold, ball gag, cock rings, shackles, rope, paddle, butt plugs, vibrators, a flogger, and on and on, like something out of *Fifty Shades*. Okay, this proves they like a bit of kink, but it doesn't prove they strangled those girls.

I pick up an oversized black wallet and zip it open to see several silk scarves in various colors folded nice and neat. Three of the four girls were strangled with silk scarves. This is good.

Adam kneels down beside me and pulls open a panel in the bottom of the trunk. Inside the compartment lay several flash drives. He grins at me as he takes one and walks it over to the wall mounted TV. He slides it in the port and turns on the television and there it is in full color—the sex tapes with Scott and Ted and the girls.

Adam asks, "How much you want to bet this is why my

brother was over at Ted's house that night? He knew Ted gave the Garners these videos."

I nod because it is a solid hypothesis. Scott and Ted were getting freaky with young women. Ted took it one step further, giving out these videos to the Garners. Scott found out and went over to confront him... Of course, that doesn't explain why Scott had a knife on him.

Honestly, I don't care why Scott was over at Ted's house that night and I probably will never know. Any way you look at it, Scott and Ted were both wrong.

"Then the Garners watch these and they get off on them," Adam continues with his thoughts, "and that's how they pick their victims."

I pick up the remaining three flash drives. "Let's see what's on these."

The first one contains porn—gay, straight, and BDSM stuff. The second one contains the Garner's doing freaky things to each other right here in this room. It's not the freaky things that bother me, I mean to each their own, but when I see several clips of them practicing erotic asphyxiation with their hands and with scarves, that's just too close for comfort.

The third drive contains them with other people—women, men, young, old—but it's not filmed here, it's filmed someplace else, and I make a mental note to see if they own any other properties.

"Look at that," Adam whispers, mashing his finger to the screen.

In the video the room is dark and I squint my eyes, studying, and it only takes a few seconds for me to realize it's one of the strangled girls. She's the one holding the silk scarf, wrapping it around Mrs. Strangler's throat.

I watch as Mr. Strangler brings his wife close to orgasm

orally and right before she reaches the peak, the girl tightens the scarf. Mrs. Strangler slowly loses consciousness, and right as she's about to pass out, the girl loosens the scarf and Mrs. Strangler's entire body arches off the bed with the orgasmic release.

Still watching the screen, Adam swallows. "Holy shit."

Yeah, holy shit indeed.

"Evidence, lab results, search warrants. We just accomplished what all the detectives on this haven't been able to," Adam says as he removes the flash drive and puts it back. "What we're doing right now, this is definitely the way to go."

I know and I agree. I haven't been this excited in a very long time.

"So what now?" He asks. "We take Mr. and Mrs. Garner?"

I laugh. "No. This is merely step one. Step two is that we begin following them and learning their routine. I also want to check into other properties that they may own."

Adam's excitement deflates a little. "So we could still be at this weeks from now?"

I look at his dejected face, and I'm not quite sure what he expected. Did he think we were going to do something tonight? "Yes, it could be weeks before we're ready to make a move."

"We're not going to stop, though, right?"

I study his expression and what I see there reminds me too much of myself. Interest. Eager. Curiosity. Impatience. All of that coupled with the intellect to understand the grand scope and the necessity for a plan.

"No, we're not going to stop," I assure him.

44

EARLY THE NEXT morning, Tommy rumbles up on his motorcycle, and I'm already outside waiting. He smiles at me as he hands me an extra helmet. "Ready?"

"Absolutely." I snap on the helmet, swing my leg over behind him, and take my time sliding my hands and arms to settle around his firm stomach.

He pulls away and through my neighborhood, winding through town, and takes back roads all the way to our zip line adventure. I don't like it when he gets on the Interstate. It reminds me of that time he nearly killed us with his recklessness.

The back roads, though, are the best. The curves and hills, the dips and play of shadows, the trees and acres of empty land, the sun and crisp air, and the smell of clean country. But my favorite part is when I close my eyes and let my arms elevate beside me with my fingers stretched wide and open, and I breathe, just breathe, and forget about my entire life.

Yes, that is my favorite part.

An hour later we pull into a gravel parking lot and park between a van and a truck. We take our helmets off, and before I'm even off the bike, Tommy's grabbing me and kissing me, and eagerly, I kiss him back.

"I plan on doing a lot of that today," he tells me.

Me, too.

We make our way across the parking area and over to where the office sits. Tommy made a reservation, and after checking us in, we go with a small squeaky voiced girl to get suited up.

After demonstrating how we should attach the harness and tether, the squeaky girl comes to check my gear first before moving on to Tommy where she takes entirely too much time pulling and tugging and "checking" his gear, too.

When she leans down to inspect God-knows-what between his legs, I move in. "He's got it. Let's go."

Tommy laughs, and I roll my eyes.

Outside the squeaky girl walks us through the safety procedures, detailing how to clip and unclip the karabiners on the zip-lines, and she giggles as Tommy demonstrates the techniques.

Finally, she nods us up the first ladder, and when I glance back, I see her staring at Tommy's butt. I turn fully to look at her, or rather glare, and she quickly spins away to head back into the office.

Tommy gives me playful nudge up the ladder. "Go, you gorgeous jealous girlfriend."

"I'm not jealous."

"Mm, hm."

Okay, maybe I am.

A few minutes later I'm standing high in the trees on a platform staring down at Tommy climbing up the ladder. I unclip the karabiner from my harness and onto the wire while I wait. He glances up at me, making a face.

Making faces at someone is not something I do, but I go with it, making one back, and Tommy laughs. God, I love his laugh.

He reaches the platform and clips on before grabbing the chin strap of my helmet and tugging me in. He gives me three quick kisses on the cheek. "I said I was going to be doing a lot of that today."

"Sounds good to me." With a smile, I turn away, kick my feet out and zoom fifty yards or so over to the next platform.

My shoes hit the wood planks and I turn to watch him zipping toward me. As he does, he lets out a silly Tarzan yell that echoes through the trees.

"You're an idiot," I yell back, and he laughs.

He comes in for a landing, and this time I tug him in for three quick kisses.

And on it goes, zipping from platform to platform—laughing, yelling, making faces, quick kisses, and simply being in the moment. It's a side of me I don't recognize, but I like it.

A couple of hours later, I zip in for our final landing, purposefully body slamming him into a pile of leaves. We roll around laughing and he tugs me to my feet. He slings his arm over my shoulders, and with our harnesses still on, we make our way over to the squeaky girl who is now collecting equipment.

As she takes Tommy's harness, he pulls me in for a delicious kiss, ending it with, "You are the bestest girlfriend in all the land."

Playfully, I roll my eyes, more than aware squeaky girl is watching us.

Tommy swats my butt, nodding toward the picnic area. "Grab us a seat, I'll get ice cream."

I've been smiling so much that my cheeks actually hurt, and while I find us a spot to sit, I work my jaw back and forth and give it a massage.

Over to the left, a big family stands in a clump, all decked out in their gear, listening to a worker give them procedures like the squeaky girl did with me and Tommy.

Way in the woods, I hear voices of others as the zip and zing through the trees.

To the right, a couple laughs at something their kid just said.

Maybe I should bring my family here. I think this would be good for all of us. To get away and simply have fun.

Tommy hands me a cone as he swings his leg over the wooden bench to sit beside me. For a few minutes, we don't speak as we lick our way through two scoops of double fudge chocolate.

When I glance over, I see him smiling a little at the couple and the kid.

"This was fun," I say.

Still, with the smile, he swipes his pinky through the ice cream, smears it on my nose, and then leans in to sloppily lick it off.

"Hey!" Laughing, I return the favor, smearing his ear.

"I like you like this," he says a few seconds later.

I like myself like this, too. "The other parts, though, do you like those, too?" And when did I start caring about such things?

"Every peculiar thing about you." He gives one single nod. "Without a doubt."

"And I you," I say, and we share yet another smile.

A few minutes later, we're throwing our napkins away

and making our way back across the gravel lot to his bike. As we backtrack through the country roads, I close my eyes and lift my face to the afternoon sun, smiling. This is what life should be like. Fun and full of air. Light and immersed in laughter. Adventurous and untroubled.

Could this become my life? Could I always be this happy? Is it possible? Do I really need to give into that other part of me?

Sometime later, Tommy pulls up in front of my house and my mood slowly begins to dip away from the brightness of the day. I want Tommy to turn around and go back. I'm not ready.

When I don't immediately get off, Tommy shifts to look over his shoulder at me. "I have to get to work."

I nod. I know.

I swing my leg over, standing beside him now, feeling uncomfortably needy. Slowly, I unclip the helmet. What is wrong with me? This isn't like me. With a little smile, that I know comes across sad, I hand it over. "Thanks, I had a really good time."

For a second Tommy studies my face, and I glance down at the pavement beneath my running shoes. I don't want him to see whatever it is going on inside of me right now.

"Hey," he softly says, taking my hand.

Now I'm looking at his thumb tenderly tracing my middle knuckle.

"Thank you for showing me this side of you," he whispers. "I knew it was there, and I'm so happy to see it."

My gaze lifts from our joined hands to meet his blue eyes. I'm so vulnerable right now that it unsettles me. I don't want to go inside my house. I don't want Tommy to leave. I want us to go back to his apartment and cuddle on his couch.

Cuddle?

When have I ever thought that word?

"Okay." He lifts my hand and presses a warm kiss to my palm, then lays my hand over his heart. "Okay." He taps my hand. "Gotta go."

Then with that, I step back and he motors away. I stand for a few minutes, watching him like I'm in the last scene of a movie.

Thank you for showing me this side of you.

I didn't mean to. It just happened. Emotion doesn't come easy for me. When other people talk about love and happiness, I tend to get confused. Those two words seem so foreign to me. Not that I don't experience those things, but they usually come with the comfortableness of my family. I didn't think it was in my nature otherwise, but with Tommy, it just happened.

In my back pocket, my cell buzzes and it brings me from my thoughts.

I pull it out and look to see Adam has texted me: WE STILL ON FOR TONIGHT?

And just like that, whether I want to be or not, I'm reminded of what I came from, the things I have done, and who I really am.

45

THAT NIGHT I'M sitting passenger in Adam's car, parked in a lot, watching Mrs. Garner, aka Mrs. Strangler, run a treadmill inside of a gym. She's been on that treadmill going on an hour. I'm in good shape but watching her is wearing me out.

"She looks harmless," Adam says. "But they usually do, right?"

True.

Adam keeps studying her. "What if she hasn't actually killed any of the girls? What if it was the husband?"

"That's why we're here. We're getting a sense of her." Narrowing my eyes I study her face as she runs on the treadmill. She's got earbuds in and is staring straight ahead at the glass that separates her from us. Her expression comes across focused. Is she thinking about sex? The girls? Her job as a nurse? The run? I wonder... "Always trust your instincts," I tell Adam.

Adam cuts me a smirk. "Is that your sensei insight?"

"No sensei. Just insight."

"So how does this work?" Adam asks next.

"How does what work?"

"Do we take her when she comes out? How do we take her? Do we throw her in the trunk?"

I've got my work cut out for me with this one. "We don't do anything. We're just watching. I never said we were taking her tonight."

"You're not doubting her guilt, are you? What about everything we found?"

I don't bother reminding him that seconds ago he was doubting her guilt. "What about it? In actuality, we have no solid proof. It's not like we've actually seen them kill one of the girls." This is a fact I point out, though my instincts tell me they're guilty.

With a sigh that comes out more of a grunt, Adam says, "Whatever."

I'm not dealing with this back and forth with Adam. He either does this my way or not. "You know what?" I nod to his ignition. "We're out of here."

"No, wait."

I shake my head. "We're done. Let's go."

Adam doesn't move and something inside the car shifts. His anxious mood slowly transitions into something else. Something thoughtful and contemplative, and I wait to see what he says.

Several silent seconds go by as he keeps watching Mrs. Strangler on the treadmill and then he quietly asks, "How many times before have you done this?"

By "done this" I know exactly what he means, and I'm not answering that question.

"When you saw me stab Ted and you helped me clean up, you were so calm and level headed. It's been bugging me, and the more I get to know you, the more I realize you know too much about all of this. This territory is beyond familiar for you."

He's right about that, but still, I say nothing.

Adam's hands slide up to his steering wheel and then down both sides. "It's okay. I guess it doesn't really matter. I'll respect your privacy."

"You're not ready," I quietly tell him.

He shifts then, to look at me in the dark car. "I think it's more you're not ready. I can sit here and tell you another sob story about my alcoholic father, but something I haven't told you about is the time he came home drunk to just me. Mom wasn't there and neither was Scott. He was laying in his own vomit, passed out, and all I could think about was all the times he hit Scott, and Scott took it. And so I started kicking him and kicking him, and it felt so good and powerful. For the first time in my life, I felt like I was getting back at my asshole father. I felt like I was getting retribution for my whole family. Like I was finally in control. That was years ago, and ever since, I've been trying to feel that way again. That is why I decided to end his life when he asked. But the truth is, I would've done it if he didn't ask me."

And that's why Adam stabbed Ted. He wanted to feel that power again.

"I've never told anyone any of that. But there's something going on inside of me and I need to let it out. Sometimes I wonder if I have a monster in me. You say I'm not ready, but I am. You need to give me a chance."

A "monster" in him. I've always thought of the people I target as the monsters, never myself. But the reality is, I do have one. I have a monster, too.

46

"**T**HANK YOU FOR this," Adam tells me, slowly circling the bed centered in the Strangler's room.

Sprawled across the mattress lay Mrs. Strangler, her arms and legs tied to the bedposts with ropes taken from their sex trunk. On the television plays one of the tapes featuring the dead girls. So poetic.

"Are you ready?" I ask Adam.

"I am."

Gagged with a ball, Mrs. Strangler's wide eyes flick between me and Adam. "Look at her trying to figure it all out."

Adam points to the screen. "We're here because of what you did to them."

Mrs. Strangler begins violently shaking her head, moaning around the ball.

Adam crawls onto the bed, positioning his knees to one side of her hips. He takes the scarf he's holding and slowly wraps it around her neck. I've never watched before. I've never stood by and been a witness. I've never seen the moment of truth from this viewpoint. "How do you feel?" I whisper.

Adam wraps the scarf again. "I feel fantastic. I feel powerful."
He glances over at me. "I feel bonded."

My whole body seems to elevate like my soul is floating away
from my bones and my muscles, and I don't breathe as I stare at
his grip on the silk scarf and wait to see if he'll do it.

Adam keeps his eyes on me as he slowly begins tightening the
scarf.

I come awake, but I don't open my eyes. My body feels
like it did in the dream, elevated and hovering away from
my skin. I set something in motion bringing Adam in.
Everything he does I am now responsible for. I am now
connected to. I am now burdened with.

It seems we both have darkness blanketing the inside of
us. I've learned to control mine, to channel mine. I've
thought about cosmic balance before. Maybe it isn't a
mistake Adam and I were brought together. We were meant
to meet. I was meant to help him, to teach him, to show him
how to control the "monster" living inside of him.

47

THE NEXT MORNING I wake up. I smile at Daisy in the bathroom. I dress. I make Justin scrambled eggs for breakfast. I give every pretense of being a normal teenage girl.

But last night and following Mrs. Strangler was no pretense. Just like breaking into her home. Adam and me, we did it together, and the more we're together the more he learns my truths. My reality.

Victor steps from the office, his phone to his ear. "Lane, weren't you with Adam last night?"

I glance up from the skillet and Justin's eggs. "Yes."

Victor waggles the phone. "It's his mom. He never came home. Wait—" Victor presses the phone to his ear. "Never mind, he just walked in." My stepdad mumbles a goodbye and hangs up. He looks at me again. "What did you two do?"

I shrug. "The usual. Hung out."

"What time did you get home?"

"Around ten or so." Because that's what time Mrs. Strangler started her night shift at the hospital and we ended our following.

Victor blows out a breath. "Looks like Adam's in trouble. I can't believe he's causing his mom an issue right now. Not with everything she's dealing with."

I can't either...

"Any idea where he went after he dropped you off?" Victor asks.

I scoop the eggs onto a plate and hand it to Justin. "No clue." But I'm going to find out.

I watch as Justin squeezes mustard onto his eggs, and with a grimace, I grab my phone and head upstairs. My brother likes the weirdest stuff.

YOU OKAY? HEARD YOU JUST GOT HOME, I text Adam when I'm in my room.

YEAH, I FELL ASLEEP IN MY CAR.

Where the hell did he fall asleep in his car? We live roughly twenty minutes from each other. What, he was so tired after he dropped me that he pulled over and took a nap? I don't buy it.

My phone rings and I pick up but before I can say hello, Adam says, "That was a lie. It's what I told my mom. She's mad, but she'll get over it."

"Okay, so where were you?"

"You know, I've been thinking all night about the imbalances in the world and how many ways we can right them."

I don't like that he uses my terminology. "Adam, where did you go?"

"We can right them with our own hands. Just thinking about it makes the world feel real. And exciting. Like for the first time in my life I'm eager to get up and start my day."

"Adam—"

"Okay, okay. I went to the hospital where our nurse works."

"You did *what*?"

"I wanted to see her interacting and stuff. I wanted to see her in her own environment."

My eyes close and I tell myself to keep calm. "There are cameras in hospitals."

"I know. I know. I was careful. Plus I already hacked the hospital's system and cross-posted any feeds with my face."

Despite my irritation, that is impressive. "Cameras aside, people saw you."

"I was in disguise. Don't worry. Don't worry. I was so wired I couldn't go back to my house. The next thing I know our nurse is clocking out and I went home. I'll be better at this, I promise. I won't do anything like that again. Just keep me focused like you've been doing. Listen, I've got to go. We'll catch up later."

I listen to him end our call, and I glance at the clock on my phone. Mrs. Strangler works the night shift and leaves at eight in the morning. It's 8:04. There's no way that timing makes sense. Adam just lied to me.

48

THAT AFTERNOON ON my way to my Patch and Paw shift, I decide to swing by the Strangler's condominium building. I roll through the parking lot, looking for the nurse's black Kia and end up rolling right back out.

I tell myself it's not strange her car isn't home. She's probably out running errands. Still, I find myself heading to the hospital and circling through the staff parking lot, and right there it is—her black Kia. Son of a bitch.

Mrs. Garner either never went home or she's already back working someone else's shift. Adam was here last night. Could be a coincidence, but probably is not.

WHERE ARE YOU? I text Adam.

WHY, YOU CHECKING UP ON ME?

Yes, I want to type back, but instead say, JUST BEING A FRIEND.

I'M FINE, NO WORRIES. YOU WANT TO COME OVER? I'VE...GOT A FEW IDEAS.

By "ideas" he either means about Mr. and Mrs. Strangler

or he's already sidetracked with something else. Adam needs to learn the importance of patience.

CAN'T, I HAVE TO WORK, I tell him.

OKAY, SEE YOU LATER.

He's got too much time on his hands.

I click off of text messaging and over to a browser to look up the number of the hospital. When I find it, I dial and it takes a minute or so to make it through the automated voice system. Finally, an operator answers.

"Hi," I say in my most friendly voice. "I'm calling for Nurse Garner. She works in the surgical ward."

"Hold please."

Muzak comes on and I don't stop staring at her car while I wait. Maybe her car was having problems and she took an Uber home. Or maybe a friend took her home. Or maybe I'm right and she's in there right now working an extra shift. I'm trying really hard not be paranoid and suspicious, but if she's not here, then something's going on.

No, Adam wouldn't do something to Mrs. Garner. Not without me.

The operator comes back on. "I'm sorry, she's not here. May I take a message?"

I don't bother saying no and instead click off. Okay, let's say Adam did do something. Where would he have put her bo—?

No.

No-no-no.

I head straight to Patch and Paw, and I'm out of my Jeep before it's fully turned off. On these afternoon shifts, I typically go straight in the front door, but today I go around the back—the same way I came in with Adam when we disposed of Ted's body.

I come to a stop at the security pad and I remember that

night. Adam was standing right beside me. He could've easily seen me punch in the code. I stare at the pad and the area around it, but nothing seems odd.

Quickly, I type in my code and I walk right in the back door.

"Hey, Lane," Dr. O'Neal greets me, her usual grin in place.

I give her a slight nod of acknowledgment and head straight to the incinerator room. As usual, it's empty and I flip the latch on the crematorium and open the door. A light automatically comes on and illuminates gray ashes and bone fragments, all of which weren't here yesterday.

Putting on gloves, I take the broom and sweep it out, saving a few of the bone fragments. After I put the ashes into a box, I take one of the bones and disappear into the lab. One of the techs stands over to the right, testing several vials of blood.

I don't think twice about stepping up to a microscope and sliding a chunk of bone underneath.

"What do you have there?" The tech asks.

"Just something I found in my yard." I dial the knobs to my specification and give the bone a good study. Animal bones have a brick like structure and human bones have more of a ring-like structure, like a tree trunk.

I zoom in, rotating the bone, and sure enough, it's human. Adam did it, he really did it, and I taught him how.

49

FTER MY PATCH and Paw shift, I go straight to Adam's house and ring his bell. His mom answers, and she barely acknowledges me as she turns away, waving her hand up the stairs. "He's in his room. You can go on up."

This woman put up with an alcoholic, abusive husband. She now knows her oldest son, Scott, was sexing it up with minors and is connected to Ted Lowman, who everyone thinks is The Strangler. What would she think if she knew what Adam was up to? It'd either send her over the edge or retract her further into herself.

I only really know this woman, the D.A., through the media and the things Adam has told me. Somehow, though, I find myself liking her. She's a hard ass with good intentions. My kind of person. Though to my knowledge, she still has not handed over the sex tapes to the investigative team. She doesn't lose points in my eyes for that. She's banking on finding Ted without exposing Scott's connection to him.

I get it. I do. I've buried more than one secret about my family.

"You made a bad decision." This is what I say to Adam the minute I walk through his bedroom door. I like to get right to the point, and he knows exactly what I'm talking about.

He swivels away from his computer to look at me. "No, *you* are the one making ridiculous decisions."

Well, at least he didn't deny anything. I close his bedroom door. "Excuse me?"

Adam folds his arms. "Waiting weeks to make a move. Following them. Waiting. What's up with that? I didn't tell you what I had in mind because I knew you wouldn't approve."

"You're damn right I don't approve. You got rid of her because you wanted to. You wanted to see what it was like. That's what drove your actions."

Adam lifts his chin. "I was serving up justice."

"Oh, bullshit."

With a sigh, Adam turns back to his computer. "I thought we didn't have to pretend with each other."

I thought so, too.

He click-click-clicks with his mouse, closing out of (surprisingly) a website about celebrities. Adam doesn't strike me as the type to really care about that type of thing. "Okay," he says, "I should have told you. I'm sorry. I honestly didn't mean to ruin the trust between us."

I stay standing behind him, staring down at the crown of his dark curly hair. Despite what he did, I'm trying really hard to give him the benefit of the doubt. To understand. But he crossed a line, and I feel like a lesson should be in order.

Adam turns off his monitor and spins back to look up at me. "Listen, you know I killed Ted. You know I killed my dad. And now I've killed Mrs. Garner. You know a lot about me that can hurt me. I've trusted you with all of that information. This friendship with you is important to me. What do I need to do to prove that?"

"A little remorse might be nice."

Adam folds his arms again. "Why? You would know I don't mean it. I'm not sorry I killed Mrs. Garner. I didn't leave any evidence. I was careful."

"Yeah, so careful you left bones in the crematorium. You're lucky I found those bones. Anybody else could have and would have known something was up. We know every animal we cremate. You're talking about experts in the field that can look at a bone and know it's human and not animal. What don't you get about that?"

Adam smiles. *Smiles.* "But you cleaned it up, so all is good."

"You won't feel so 'good' if you get caught."

His smile falls away. "We live in a big area. The cops will think she's been taken. Or she ran off with a lover. I'm not worried about it. Her disappearance will blend in with everything else that's wrong." Adam pushes up out of his chair. "Listen, this is the nature of friendship. Sometimes we're going to agree and other times not."

He's sounding a lot like Victor saying that.

Adam crosses the expanse of his room and opens his door. "I've got stuff I want to do. I'll see you later."

Adam thinks he's got things figured out. He thinks he's untouchable. How wrong he is. A lesson is definitely in order.

50

I 'VE SPENT MY life with a wall around me, letting very few people in. I won't say all, but many of the people I have let in have disappointed me. Like Adam currently is. Tough love. Isn't that part of being a good friend? Yes, yes it is.

This is what I tell myself as I take the box containing Mrs. Garner's ashes and bones, divide them between two containers, and seal them both up.

I spend the entire night going back and forth on what to do with them. If I give the contents to the cops, then they'll raid Mr. Strangler's condominium, find his *Fifty Shades* trunk, watch the videos, and he will officially replace Ted as the number one suspect in the strangler case.

All neat and tidy.

If, however, I give the remains to Mr. Strangler, then I get to watch what he does. He'll either hand the evidence over to the cops, or he'll dispose of it and begin weaving a tale as to where his wife went.

There is a very small chance this man is not The Strangler, and if he is innocent of killing those girls, then he'll hand the ashes over. Which means I'm back to square one in my search for the real Strangler, and Adam took out an innocent woman. Unless Mrs. Garner was the sole strangler, and the mister had nothing to do with the final act.

Either way, if that's the route Mr. Garner goes, then he would be smart to clear his condo of that trunk under his bed. Surely he knows that would raise major flags.

But then that gets me to thinking that might be a smart move. Handing the ashes over and clearing his condo of that hidden trunk will make him look innocent, and then he can continue on with his strangling ways.

It's like a game of chess and this is what I love most—waiting to see what someone will do.

I'm possibly giving up The Strangler in doing this, but a lesson to Adam seems more important right now.

Which is why I ultimately decide to deliver two boxes: one to Mr. Strangler and the other to the cops.

First stop, Mr. Strangler.

51

"**I DON'T UNDERSTAND**," a fellow nurse cries into the camera. "She was such a good person. Who would do this? They're saying the killer was a pro. That doesn't make any sense. Why would a pro-killer go after Mrs. Garner?"

Pro-killer? That's a new term.

The camera switches to her condo building and the cops going in and out. Mr. Garner is nowhere to be seen, but I know he disposed of the sex toy trunk. I watched him.

I decided to deliver his present first and twelve hours later I delivered the next present to the cops. But in those twelve hours, Mr. Strangler disposed of the evidence. I followed him all the way to a landfill located a county over where he dumped the trunk, then I followed him to a local precinct where he walked right in with the box of ashes and bones under his arm.

Of course, the cops received a similar box of ashes hours after that, but I did want to see how Mr. Strangler would handle everything. Now, of course, there's a new killer on the loose. So much for the strangled girls, now there's someone running around burning people.

Oh, what trouble I stir up.

The camera pans wide to all the residents huddled outside the condominium building, staring in shock at the activity. Some are crying. A lot of people have been affected by the nurse's death. From their viewpoint, she was a good and decent person. A good and decent person who had kinky proclivities and got off on strangulation.

Honestly, I could get into a bit of kink as well. There's nothing wrong with safe exploration of desires. Of course, that line gets crossed when someone dies.

All that aside, this was all brought on by Adam's deception. He needs to know he's not untouchable. Even though there is no real evidence to link him to Mrs. Strangler's death. He did wipe the security footage and burned the body, but my point will still be made.

He should never cross me.

LESSON LEARNED, this is the text I get from Adam as I'm flipping the news to a different channel.

Good, I'm glad he thinks so. But once a liar, always a liar, and I'm not trusting him until I do a bit more digging on what he does when he's not with me.

Plus, I still need to find out if Mr. Strangler owns any other properties because on the videos there was another room. He may have disposed of that trunk, but there's another one somewhere. I know it. There is a place where he and his wife got it on with those girls. I just need to find it.

52

THE NEXT MORNING I ring the Butler's doorbell, and the D.A. swings open the door. I give her my best smile.

Distracted with her phone pressed to her ear, she waves me in with a mumbled, "Adam's gone, but you can wait in his room if you want."

I step right on in. "Thanks." Of course, I already knew Adam was gone, otherwise, I wouldn't be here.

I would be very mad at Victor if he gave someone permission to wait in my room for me, and I'm sure Adam's not going to like it either. But his feelings on the topic are not my problem.

I take the wide curving staircase two steps at a time. If I was a whistler, I'd be whistling right now. He's at the dentist, and I estimate he'll be home in thirty minutes or so. Plenty of time.

After closing his door, I go straight to his computer and type in his password. If there's one thing I've learned about people who are up to no good, they keep pictures. Way too many pictures. Or videos. Some hard copies, others electronic. Adam is just cocky enough to keep his right on his computer.

He thinks he's untouchable.

I plug in a flash drive and while it goes through the motion of copying the entire hard drive, I begin snooping. I open his picture folder and begin browsing. Family stuff, vacations, lots of the new puppy, Sally. I open one harmlessly labeled FRIENDS and begin clicking through. I come across one of Catalina, my copycat, and I pause.

She's standing with a baseball bat propped on her shoulder, dressed in track pants and a dark tee with PEE-WEE POLICE monogrammed on it. She's got her other arm looped over Adam's shoulders, dressed, too, in track pants and a black tee with the same logo. To any onlooker, they're just two friends hanging out and playing ball for a team called PEE-WEE POLICE. I suppose that makes sense. Adam's mom is the D.A. and Catalina's dad is a cop.

Yes, I suppose that makes sense, only I know Catalina used that bat to bludgeon innocent people, or a bat just like it. My copycat, right there, pals with my new friend, Adam. You can tell a lot about a person by the friends he keeps.

It hits me hard as I look at the digital image of the two of them. The deceit. I didn't mentor Adam. I didn't guide him or help him. He's known the entire time who I am. He's been using me, been lying to me, and I've played into his every move.

My mind barrels down a dark hole lined with nasty paranoia. It backtracks through the time I've had with Adam. To that moment I first met him outside of Ted's house. Adam spoke first, he initiated contact. He knew exactly who I was. He's been leading me the whole time. He staged Ted's stabbing, knowing I would find him. He showed up in Penn's court, tantalizing me with Mr. Pedophile. Adam led me to Stabber Brother. He led me to the sex tapes. All the "heart-to-hearts" we had, linking on a deeper level. The flash drive containing The Strangler information he held just out of reach. Hell, he even adopted an effing dog to connect with me.

And I followed his every move. I stepped where he wanted. I've been his puppet. He's been playing me this whole time. But to what end? To get back at me for Catalina? To get me to relax to the point of making some damaging admission? Or is there something else bigger that I'm just not seeing? I can't be sure, but I am sure he's double-crossed the wrong person.

Or perhaps I really am spiraling into the land of paranoia. Perhaps he has no clue that I knew Catalina. Perhaps my relationship with Adam is exactly as it seems—a bit of a warped friendship that is going through its shares of ups and downs. I lunge at that thought, wanting to believe it over the rest. But I don't know. I shake my head, trying to force the disconnect in my brain to link.

What I do know is that I'm officially done. I've been operating under this misguided perception that I owed him. I accidentally killed his beloved brother and I owed him, but I'm done. I've more than paid my debt. If it were anyone else, I would've been done with him a while ago.

I hear him coming up the stairs, and I quickly extract the flash drive and close down. Swiveling in his chair, I kick my legs up on his desk, and I'm browsing my phone when he walks in.

"Hey," he says, his gaze moving from me to his desk.

I smile, faking civility. "Hey."

"Um..." He takes a few steps in. "I don't really like people in my room unless I'm here."

I let my feet thud to the carpet. "Oh, sure." I stand up. "I get it." Another smile, and I begin to entertain options of how to deal with him.

Number one, I could make him disappear. The problem is, being the son of the D.A., Adam is high profile, or rather his mom is. She already had one son killed, it would look odd for two. Plus, if Adam turns up missing, I'm the first person his mom would question. I'm his new "best friend".

Number two, I could simply end our friendship. Somehow, though, I know it won't be that simple. I've taught him too much. His ego is out of control. I'm responsible if he kills or harms someone again.

Number three, I get these tables turned. Let him become my puppet, which means I need leverage. I thought the box of dust and bones would achieve that, but it seems to have made him even more of a challenge.

No, what we need is an eyewitness. Or rather a video witness. Adam said he wiped the security feed clean. If I've learned anything from being friends with Reggie, nothing is ever wiped clean.

Plus, with Adam's ego fully inflated, I suspect he kept the deleted feed. He would want to revisit it and see himself in action. I only need to find the deleted feed, and I just happen to have the contents of his computer on a flash drive in my pocket.

"Lane?"

I straighten up, realizing I'd zoned out. "Yeah, sorry."

"I said, what are you doing here?"

"Oh, nothing, I guess. Just dropped by to say hi. I mean, isn't that what *friends* do?"

In response, Adam keeps watching me. "I said I learned my lesson."

I move away from his desk and over to sit in the leather recliner situated under his bay window. "I need peace of mind you covered your tracks."

Adam moves away from the doorway, seeming more relaxed now with my intrusion. He heads over to his desk and sits in the swivel chair I just vacated. "Don't worry, I was careful."

"With the video feed, sure, but what about the actual people who saw you? You know the cops will question them."

"No thanks to you."

I ignore the jab. "You know it would've cycled around to that anyway."

"I know. I know." Adam waves a hand airily. "So what do we do, frame Mr. Garner?"

Though I'm curious to hear his plan to frame, I instead say, "*We?*" And then I chuckle. "You lost that privilege when you went behind my back."

Adam's face falls. "Are you saying you don't want to be friends anymore?"

Okay, maybe option two will work. "Yes, that is what I'm saying."

"Are you sure, because I can be a good friend to have."

His cocky remark doesn't surprise me.

"I'm sure."

The response that comes next does surprise me. I expected more cockiness or even anger or spite, not...tears. I'd like to think I can tell the difference between real and fake, and his sure come across real. I've hurt his feelings.

"If that's what you want," he mumbles.

I push myself up out of the recliner feeling, oddly

enough, remorse. I'm not sure why. He lied to me. He double-crossed me. I should feel good about this, about walking away. I expected more of a debate from him, more of a fight. Frankly, I expected not to care.

Still, I say, "Yes, that's what I want," and I walk straight from his room.

53

ALL THE WAY home I think about Adam's framing comment. With his mom being the D.A., he's got the inside scoop on a lot of things. After what happened to his brother, Adam's mom is vulnerable, and Adam knows it. I don't doubt he'll use her if need be.

I like Adam's mom. I'll need to keep an eye on the situation.

When I pull up outside of our house, Daisy and Hammond are arguing.

"Why did you lie to me?" Hammond demands.

Daisy looks away. "Because telling you wasn't going to change anything."

"I thought you were different. I thought you said the 'old you' was over."

Daisy brings her blue gaze back to his. "She is over. I swear."

Hammond heaves a thoughtful sigh. "You know what? I don't believe you."

Daisy throws her hands up. "Fine, then walk away. I don't want to be with someone who doesn't trust me."

"Okay." He runs a rough hand through his brown hair. "I'm walking away."

From my Jeep, I watch as he climbs in his dad's Maxima and drives off. Daisy walks right toward me, opens the passenger side, and gets in. With a sigh, she slouches back into the seat like she's just lost all of her bones.

"What's going on?" I ask.

She shakes her head. "Do you remember West?"

I think about that. "No, not really."

"Old boyfriend. You walked in on me giving him head?"

"Oh, yeah, that."

"Anyway, his older sister was murdered and someone cremated her. I went over to console him and now Hammond's pissed."

Murder and cremated. Talk about a small world. "You referring to that nurse? I saw it on the news."

"Yeah, that's the one."

"Does the family have any ideas of who did it?"

"West thinks it was the husband. Apparently, they were into some kinky sex shit that no one knew about. West thinks that things got out of hand and the husband burned her body and is now acting like he's innocent."

"You say no one knew about the kinky sex shit? How did they find out?"

"Some anonymous person sent photos of them doing weird stuff to each other. I don't know, whips and chains and whatever else. I mean, if that's what you want to do, go for it, right?"

"Right." And by "anonymous" person, that means Adam.

It looks like he's already started the framing. He knew exactly what his next moves were going to be. Oh, he's good. He must have gone back into the Garner's condominium, either the same day or soon after, to make copies of those drives.

Closing her eyes, Daisy presses her fingers into her forehead. "The old me would've brushed this whole thing off and found a million reasons why Hammond sucks. But instead of that, I'm sitting here right now thinking about how happy I am when I'm with him."

Even though you admitted to role-playing? I want to say but keep that to myself.

54

L ATER THAT NIGHT, Adam calls me, and I'm not surprised to see his name on the I.D. I knew I wasn't going to be able to just end our friendship. He says, "You know, I've been thinking, it was kind of a dick move sending my mom those videos of Scott and Ted."

"You know why I did it," I remind him. She needed to stop probing into Scott's death. I couldn't help it that those videos then cycled around to being connected to The Strangler.

"You shouldn't play games like that."

Yeah, he's one to talk.

"But in the interest of friendship," he says, "or, lack thereof, I think I should probably tell you that I've been keeping notes on everything about you."

"Really," I say.

"Just so you know you're not the only one with leverage should...things go south."

Adam has no idea what door he just opened with that threat. I don't bother responding and instead, hang up. From my pocket, I pull out the flash drive loaded with the contents of his computer. I plug it into my laptop.

Aside from the picture of him and Catalina, time to see what all is really here. Adam is a computer nerd, and the one mistake computer people make is that they keep an e-version of everything.

Adam has stepped over way too many lines with me, and he'll keep right on doing so until I have solid evidence he can't beat. Something that will make him back down altogether. That's the only way he'll fall back into place.

I know what it's like to want to rebalance an unbalanced world, but sometimes once you open that door and walk through, it's way too easy to stroll through it again. That's what has happened to Adam, and I need to find a way to shut that door again.

It takes me several hours to go through all his files, videos, and photos. With being Catalina's friend, I'm surprised not to find Masked Savior information and I begin to doubt if he knew who she really was. If he knew she was my copycat.

I also find nothing on me and am surprised there, too. I was expecting to come across buried photos dating back to the days when Catalina followed me, but again nothing.

It's like he truly became this other person since meeting me, and I do not take that as a compliment at all.

I begin to doubt if he has been playing me this whole time. I don't know. I truly don't know.

What I do find is the security feed from the hospital, the real feed, with pictures of him and Mrs. Garner. Them talking, them walking down a hall, them disappearing into an elevator. They emerge out of the garage and vanish off camera before re-emerging. I watch as they laugh, almost like they know each other, then he hands her a water bottle.

She uncaps it, takes a swig, and seconds later, slowly slumps to the floor. The next time I see them, Adam is loading her into the trunk of his car.

Laughing, almost like they knew each other...

I file that thought away and screenshot several clips before printing them out. Whatever she drank obviously knocked her out. But did it kill her? That I'm not sure of.

Still, I put the photos in an envelope, seal it up, and neatly print his name on the outside. It's after midnight when I drive them over to his house and leave them in his mailbox.

I follow it with a text: CHECK YOUR MAIL

55

THE NEXT MORNING my phone rings and I see Adam's name come across the screen.

"You think you're funny?" He demands.

"No, I don't."

"How did you get those clips?"

"I have my ways, and you need to know that."

"You bitch, you were on my computer when you were in my room. I trusted you!"

"And I you."

He scoffs. "You think you're so clean in all of this?"

"Yes, actually I do because I don't keep important things that could be found." I don't keep things that tie me to my deeds. I don't make the mistake of keeping "trophies".

"You're messing with the wrong person," he says in a tone, deep and threatening.

"Ditto."

Adam huffs out an unamused laugh. "Wow, I see it now. You can't be reasoned with. A relationship with you is pointless."

If he means I can't be controlled, then bully to him for finally figuring that out.

"You do what you want when you want. Is that it?" He asks.

Pretty much. "It's all about choices, good and bad, and you've made too many bad ones."

"So, what, you're the judge and jury?"

I shrug. "If you wish."

"I thought we were friends."

My search for someone to connect with has officially ended. I've beyond learned my lesson. This part of me, it's a solo operation. If Adam doesn't get that now, then he's going to force me to take alternative action.

"Consider us officially over," he says.

I nod. "Agreed."

I only have myself to blame for this thing with Adam. Maybe I'm trying too hard at this normal life thing and having friends. Maybe I need to revert back to what I know best. Me.

Adam reminds me of a wounded animal, and everyone knows what you do with a wounded animal. You put them out of their misery.

56

THAT NIGHT I trot up the steps toward our front door and halfway up, I pause. Something's not right. I backtrack down the steps and glance up at our three-floor home. I look to the bottom where the basement lies, the first floor with the main area, and the top floor where our bedrooms are located.

Where are all the lights? There's always lights on. And why are all the curtains drawn? Victor never closes the curtains.

I glance up the block and down at all the other homes in our neighborhood to find their lights on. I turn and survey the cul-de-sac and the vehicles parked in their spots. Nothing seems out of place. There are a few extra vehicles, but that's normal.

I take a few steps to the left and look down our side yard. I look up at all of our windows, dark from this angle, too, with blinds and curtains drawn.

Yes, something is definitely not right. I cross out of our yard and back toward the driveway, and lifting up on my toes, I peak into the garage window and see Victor's SUV there. He's home.

I pull my phone out of my back pocket and shoot off a quick: DAD, ARE YOU IN THE HOUSE? WHY IS EVERYTHING SO DARK?

I wait several minutes, but no return text comes back. That's not like him. He always returns my texts. I shoot Daisy one next, then Justin, and I get nothing back from them either.

Shit, this isn't good. I wonder if this is how my victims feel—trapped, confused, hopeless.

Well, I might be confused but I refuse to feel the other two. I backtrack to my Jeep and from my Aikido bag, I get my bokken. The last time I really used it was with Catalina, and that memory should unsettle me, but it serves only to bolster me.

With it gripped tightly in my hand, I make my way back up the front steps. As quietly as I can, I slip my key in and click it left, slowly opening the door.

It's completely dark in here, with only a sliver of moonlight trickling in through the blinds across the room. I step further in, and something to my right shifts. I don't wait to see, to ask, to nothing, I swing out with my bokken and hear a satisfying crack.

"Shit!" Someone screams.

All the lights flick on and people jump out of everywhere shouting a resounding, "Surprise!"

It takes me a second to register the birthday balloons and banner, and several people rushing to help Victor, who I just cracked with my bokken.

"Oh my God," I drop to my knees next to him. "I'm so sorry."

With a grimace, he grips his forearm. "Glad to know all those Aikido lessons have paid off."

Someone runs to get an ice pack. Someone else helps Victor up. I walk with him over to the couch. Then the ice pack appears and I take it, laying it gently over his forearm.

Now several minutes later the party has resumed and I'm still sitting beside Victor while I eye the people packed into our downstairs. I spy neighbors, kids I went to school with, my family, Patch and Paw workers (including the annoying doctor), the D.A., Adam, and Tommy.

Tommy's standing over in the corner, idly listening to my neighbor yammer on and on, wearing the same "kill me now" expression that I know I must be sporting.

I don't know who thought a party was a good idea, but I doubt it was my family. They know me well enough to know, I don't do parties.

Victor shifts the ice pack off and gives his arm a little twist. I cringe. "Any better?"

He smiles. "I'll survive. You were certainly freaked, huh?"

"To put it lightly."

"Adam was dead set on this," Victor tells me, "and I didn't have the heart to say no."

So, Adam's the culprit. "When did he plan this?"

"A while ago."

Before we parted ways then, which puts him here out of obligation. I glance across the room and into the kitchen where he's currently serving himself from the buffet of wings, chips, and hot dogs. At least he got the food right. I'm all about a good mustard dog.

He glances up then, as if sensing my gaze, but he doesn't give me any sign of recognition or acknowledgment. That's fine. He can go through the motions of this party and then be out of my life.

"Might want to smile," Victor mumbles, "and at least fake a party face."

"You're right. I'm sorry." I take a sip of punch that someone brought me, and I make my lips curve up. These people are here for me and that's nice, even if Adam's the one who organized it.

While I understand birthday parties are a part of human ritual, I've never understood the need for them. It's just a bunch of people standing around waiting on a cake to be cut and to make an exit. I mean, who really wants to go to a birthday party? Don't they have anything better to do? I know I do.

In my back pocket, my phone buzzes and I slip it out to see.

CAREFUL, YOUR FACE MIGHT FREEZE THAT WAY. This is the text that comes in from Tommy and it brings a genuine smile to my lips. I wish he was over here next to me and not standing in the corner.

WANT TO SEE MY BEDROOM? I text back because I need a break from this scene.

UM...

MEET ME AT THE STAIRS. I turn to Victor. "I'm going to show Tommy the upstairs. I won't be long."

He nods. "Okay, and when you get a chance, I'd like to meet him. I hear you two are official?"

I put my punch down on the coffee table. "Where'd you hear that?"

"Adam."

Of course.

"Only a few minutes," Victor says. "We have candles to blow out and a cake to cut."

"Oh joy."

Victor laughs and gives me a little nudge. "I'll hold down the fort."

As I make my way around the crowd and not through it, someone cranks up the music. I hear a *whoop-whoop* and Dr. O'Neal starts twerking. Good God.

With Tommy right behind me, I can't get up the stairs fast enough. I need a break from the party, sure, but I need a groping session with him even more.

I swing open my bedroom door, not bothering to hide my impatience, and as soon as I step inside I turn to grab Tommy, and he pushes me up against the wall instead. With his foot, he kicks the door closed and his mouth crashes to mine.

His fingers thread through my hair, gripping tight, and we're so on the same page. There are no soft kisses. It's lips and tongue and teeth. When he pulls on my hair, I moan, and he takes that as a cue to move forward.

He lifts me up by my hips, and I wrap my legs around him, squeezing hard. He slides his hands around to cup my backside, and I arch out from the wall.

My hands wrap around his shoulders, and my fingertips dig into the muscles there, and when he presses into me, a fiery need barrels down my spine.

Tommy pushes firmer into me, and I cling to him, completely wrapped up in him. As I match his kiss, it wrings every bit of myself out of me, and I'm replaced with something softer.

Our kiss slows then, going from demanding to exploratory. His breath comes warm against my mouth, and I relish every slide of our tongues. My arms loosen and now that I'm not locked against him, the rise and fall of our breath brings on a sensual rocking as we rub against each other.

All thoughts are abandoned as he slips his hand under my shirt and up my spine, stroking me, touching me, and I melt into him, stretching like a cat. Now, this is how I'd rather be spending my birthday.

I open lazy eyes to look at him. I wish we had the luxury of taking this further, but my party rages on downstairs.

As if on cue, Daisy bangs on my door. "Zip it up and get back downstairs. Cake time."

My legs disengage from Tommy's hips, and he takes a second to look around my room. He's seen it before when he broke in and took my serial killer journals, but that's ancient history now. That was back when was trying to figure out what I was hiding. Now, though, he thinks The Decapitator was my uncle. Everyone thinks that.

"Looks different from this angle."

"What angle is that?" I tease.

His lips twitch. "The angle that says I'm allowed to be in here."

I open the door and Daisy is right there, grinning. She looks from me to Tommy and back to me. "Aaawww. Lane and Tommy sitting in a tree. K-i-s-s-i-n-g."

Rolling my eyes, I give her a little shove, but I'm happy to see her like this. She's been so to herself lately.

Back downstairs, Dr. O'Neal has thankfully stopped twerking and Adam is standing on a stool. When he spies me, he sticks his fingers in his mouth and whistles, and everyone quiets down.

He clears his throat, and I'm more than curious to see what he says. "As you all know, we are here today to celebrate Lane's birthday. I've only known Lane for a little while, but our friendship has made a *lasting* impression on me."

This gets a few chuckles from the crowd.

"The thing about a true friend is that they are always honest with each other and they can not only appreciate but also see past differences. They can fight and still forgive. Lane, in the short time we've known each other, I've learned so much from you." Adam lifts his punch glass. "So here's to you on this special day."

Everyone cheers and toasts, and I put yet another smile on my face, but my gaze never leaves Adam's as he takes a sip of his punch, his gaze never leaving mine as well. There's something calculating in his stare, and I recognize the depths. He and I share more than one secret, secrets that I'm afraid are going to force one of our hands.

I'm kidding myself if I think it's as simple as cutting ties. This party right here is proof. And with Victor and the D.A. over on the couch, talking and laughing, I have a feeling our lives are only going to become more and more entwined.

Dealing with Adam requires finesse. I can't just make him go away. It's not like he's some homeless kid that no one will miss. If I am going to permanently take action, and I'm not completely to that point yet, but if I do get to that point, it'll need to be pinned on someone else.

As I think all of this, I'm still staring into his eyes, and I know that shrewd look. He's thinking the exact same thing.

Daisy slides up beside me. "What's going on with the two of them?"

My gaze slides off of Adam and over to Victor and the D.A. "You know they were friends in high school, right? I think they probably even dated."

Daisy's face hardens. "What is Dad doing? Mom's not even been dead a year."

"They're just talking."

The D.A. slides her hand over Victor's knee and gives it a little squeeze, and they both laugh.

"What the hell?" Daisy starts to take a step forward, and I grab her arm.

"Leave them alone. Let Dad have some laughter."

Daisy jerks her arm from my grasp. "This was Mom's house. He needs to show respect. Plus, look at her. Mom was way prettier and better and everything."

"Mom wasn't perfect."

Daisy shoots me an angry look. "Yes, she was."

I keep my calm. "No, she wasn't."

"I want to be exactly like her."

"No, you don't." I don't bother reminding her that she fought with Mom on a daily basis.

Daisy eyes me hard. "What's that supposed to mean?"

"Just that...there're things you don't know." As soon as it's out of my mouth, I regret it.

The anger fades from my sister's face, and it's replaced by something tragic and confused. "Wh..." her blue eyes tear up. "What are you talking about?"

Our little brother bounds up beside us, cell phone in hand. "Birthday selfie!"

We indulge Justin, leaning down into the frame, and he snaps a pic that he then forwards to both of us. Over the years our pictures mirror the same thing—Justin with his little boy glow, Daisy and her sweet grin, and me and my blank expression. But this time when I pull up the pic, Justin's the one with the sweet grin, I've managed a soft glow, and Daisy has taken on the blankness.

A blankness I caused.

57

DAISY LOOKS UP *from the bloody knife she holds in her hand.*

"What did you do?" I whisper.

"There are no words to describe it. The sound of the blade cutting in. The sound of the screaming. I was someone else."

My eyes open, and I stare once again at the ceiling of my bedroom. It's daylight out and a quick check of my bedside clock shows seven in the morning. That's two hours later than I usually sleep. I hear my family moving around beyond my door, and I wonder if they think I'm dead.

I don't know why I'm having so many dreams and begin to question my clear conscious theory. Maybe a conscious—clear or otherwise—has nothing to do with sleep. Though I like thinking they're connected because I rarely dream which should mean I have nothing to feel guilty about.

I should have never told Daisy what I did about Mom, and I know it was selfish. But I want someone else to hate Mom as much as I do. I want someone else to realize she was not a good person.

And that dream, obviously made up, is still unsettling.

Daisy stayed by my side the rest of the birthday party, bugging me to tell her what I knew. I finally got rid of her during clean up and came up here to my room. When I locked my door, she started texting me. Texts I didn't return.

I'm going to have to come clean, with at least something. A little something. Enough to satisfy and justify my comment.

Sitting up in bed, I swing my legs over and it comes to me. I know exactly what I'm going to tell her.

I find Daisy in the bathroom brushing her teeth, and picking up my toothbrush, I begin brushing mine. Downstairs I hear Victor and Justin in the kitchen, so I know we have privacy.

Daisy watches me in the mirror, scrubbing away, eyeing me as I brush mine. Her blue eyes, so much like Mom's, narrow in on me, and I know she's pissed. I divert my gaze, staring at myself for a few seconds while I gather my thoughts. My tongue feels unusually thick, like if I speak it'll come out mumbled. I don't know how she's going to take this, but here it goes.

I spit out my paste and rinse, and she does the same. I take a few seconds to wash my face with cool water and dry, then with a glance over my shoulder, I close the door, and I lean up against the counter and fold my arms. She's got the vent on from her recent shower, and I know the white noise will cover our voices.

"What I'm about to tell you stays between you and me." I look her dead in the eyes. "You understand?"

She wipes her hands on a gray towel, then turns, matching my stance against the counter. I study her expression, seeing exactly what I was hoping for—maturity and understanding.

"Yes," she quietly assures me. "I understand."

I take a breath. Here goes nothing. "Back when we were cleaning out the house after Mom died, I came across a key to a locker at the Dunn Loring Station. I didn't tell anyone about the key because I had this weird sense that Mom was hiding something. I went to that locker and I opened it, and inside I found a box. In that box were pictures and love letters between her and a man who wasn't Dad." Some of that is true, some is false, but it's enough to satisfy my comment from last night.

Daisy doesn't react. She just keeps looking at me, and the air between us becomes blanketed by her silence. "Do you still have them?" she finally speaks.

"No," I truthfully say. "I burned them in the cremation room at Patch and Paw."

"So you're saying Mom was having an affair?"

"Yes, that's what I'm saying."

With a sigh, she drops her gaze and I wait a few seconds, trying to get a read on her. Interesting enough, I can't. I can't tell if she's angry or confused or what.

I say, "You understand this has to stay between you and me. It will kill Dad if he ever finds out."

Daisy lifts her eyes to mine, then she turns and grips the edge of the sink. She spends a few seconds looking down at the drain and I watch her, trying again to gauge her mood, but I can't tell what she's thinking.

"What a bitch," she says, and it takes me off guard. I wasn't expecting that. She pushes away from the sink and turns to look at me again. "Who was it?"

"I don't know," I say, lying again. "The love letters were signed with initials and first names only. And the pictures, I didn't recognize the man."

"Someone from the FBI?"

I shrug. "I don't know."

"Do you think he lives around here?"

Another shrug. "I've told you everything I know."

Daisy blows out another breath, shaking her head, and I see it then—the disappointment, the hate. "I really don't like Mom right now."

"I know. Daisy, you can't say any—"

She holds up her hand. "You can count on me, I won't say a word."

I nod. "Okay." I wait to see if she wants to say anything else, but she doesn't speak, so I think things are over. I go to open the door, and Daisy stops me to give me a quick hug.

"Thank you for trusting me with that information."

I hug her back, wondering how that conversation would have gone if I had told her the rest.

Daisy pulls back, and a small beautiful smile softens her face. "Despite all of this, do you think Mom would be proud of the people we're becoming?"

That question seems to come out of nowhere, but I quickly reply, "Yes, she would be especially proud of the fact we're friends now." That much I know is true.

Daisy chuckles. "Yeah, look at us."

A smile inches into my lips. "Yeah, look at us."

58

THE THING ABOUT being friends with someone is that you learn their schedule. Like that Reggie is a night owl and will happily text you back at two in the morning. Or that Tommy works every Tuesday night at Whole Foods past closing at eleven to count stock. Or that Adam has dinner with his Uncle Judge Penn the first and third Wednesday of every month.

We haven't seen, texted, or talked to each other since the birthday party weeks ago and, truthfully, I'm in Penn's courtroom hoping to run into Adam. Hoping to look into his eyes and get another read on him.

Except for this Wednesday, he doesn't show.

In my Jeep, I backtrack to his house and do a slow drive by, but his old Chevy is gone. I do spy Sally, the puppy, cheerily barking and doing her watchdog job. Good job, Sally.

I've been doing checks on Mr. Strangler and decide today is as good as any. I make my way across town to the building where Mr. Strangler works, and I spy his vehicle parked in the lot. I do a visual sweep of the area, and I see the same unmarked car I've seen a few times now.

Mr. Strangler is under surveillance.

Next, I go to the condominium building where Mr. Strangler lives. Since I don't have Adam and the D.A. as my inside source, I've been keeping up with the case through my new inside source—Daisy and her old boyfriend, West, the younger brother of Mrs. Garner.

I don't know all the ins and outs, but the investigation is still wide open. I imagine it has everything to do with recent mishandling of evidence within the county. The team of detectives wants to dot every "i" and cross every "t". They can't afford any more flubs.

All that aside, I imagine Mr. Strangler is laying way low. I still have no leads on additional properties he may be connected to, and I refuse to call Reggie. But the thing about laying low is that deviants eventually surface. They can't stay low for long. They need whatever it is that drives them.

This I understand.

Slowly, I pull through the condominium parking lot, my eyes popping across all the vehicles. I don't see any surveillance here.

I do spy Adam's car, though, over in the corner under a tree. My Jeep slows as I eye his vacated Chevy. He's up in the Garner's condo right now, and I showed him how to get up there. What is he doing?

A part of me wants to sit back and see, but another nagging part tells me something's wrong about this. Why would he go up in broad daylight?

Hide in plain sight. That thought comes to me and has me parking across the packed lot and behind the dumpster.

I make my way over to Adam's car and sidle up beside it,

taking a peek inside. It looks like it usually does—change in the cup holder, a toll road meter mounted to the window, a metal water bottle in the other cup holder, and a clean back seat.

I round to the trunk and using my lockpicks, I jimmy it open. I'm not sure what I expect to see, but the rolls of plastic and bags of dry cement are not it. Adam definitely has something planned.

Surely, he's not going to use Patch and Paw's cremation room again.

I had such high hopes for him, for us. I thought he was naïve, but really, I was the naïve one. He actually had me believing it was possible to have a true friend, that he and I saw the possibility in each other.

Hell, to think I almost let him completely in. The truth is, only my victims have seen the real me.

The side door to the building opens then, and Adam emerges. Or rather I know it's Adam but others would not. He looks how he did in the videos from the hospital with a ball cap, no glasses, and a fake mustache.

Carefully, I back away from his car, ducking behind an SUV to watch. He crosses the parking lot to his vehicle and climbs inside. He cranks his engine and slowly pulls through the lot and around back to where a pool sits. What is he doing?

It's quick, and if I wasn't here staring I wouldn't see what happens next. Dressed in his own disguise of a ball cap and dark shades, Mr. Garner emerges from the shadows of the trees, slips into the passenger side of Adam's car, and slides all the way down so he's not seen.

Adam begins weaving through the parking lot toward the exit, and I beeline it back over to my Jeep. I don't know where they're going, but I'm following.

I thought it before when I watched the hospital footage,

and I'm thinking it now. Adam and the nurse seemed to know each other, and from what I saw just now, he definitely knows Mr. Garner.

I follow a safe distance, glad for the heavy traffic that will hide me, and my brain begins to pick through the details. The Garners were into some kinky stuff. As evidenced by all the videos, they had multiple sex partners. Is Adam one of them? Does this all boil down to Adam being a jealous lover? Is that why he took out Mrs. Garner?

Or did he and Mr. Garner plan all of this? Did they strangle those girls, all along framing Teddy, and decide to take out the nurse because she was the only witness?

Do they plan on eventually taking me out?

But then why would Adam send those photos to the cops to implicate Mr. Garner? Too many questions...

When his car takes the on-ramp, I merge and follow. I don't know where they're going, but my gut tells me it's to the place where the girls were strangled. I'm about to find out one way or another how Mr. Strangler and Adam are connected.

I TRAIL THEM all the way to Loudoun County and into a cute little neighborhood with cottage style homes on big wooded lots. From a few lots over I watch as Adam pulls into the garage and closes the door.

The name on the mailbox says RUSK and it seems familiar. It only takes me a few seconds to piece it together. Mr. Strangler works for Rusk Engineering. This must be where clients stay when they visit the area.

No wonder I couldn't find any additional properties connected to the Garners. There are none. They've been using this, and I have to say I'm impressed with the smarts behind it. Broad daylight, cute little place corporately owned, no one would think anything odd.

Every single blind in the house is swiveled shut, so I park on the far end of the property, tucked between two enormous maple trees. For a good ten minutes, I sit and watch the place, waiting to see if there is movement.

When nothing happens, I open the door and cross over the neatly cropped grass to the white picket fence.

For a second I stand, my gloved fingers locked around a

wooden post, and I peer at the brick and wood cottage. Yes, this is where they do it. They lure their victims into this cute little place, park right there in the garage, do their erotic asphyxiation thing, load the body into the trunk, and dump it somewhere within a radius of Teddy's house, effectively pointing fingers in his direction.

Even if Adam hasn't told Mr. Garner that Ted is dead, Garner has to know Ted is currently at large. He has to know his continual dumping of bodies will only last so long. Maybe that's why Adam cremated Mrs. Garner, he and Mr. Garner wanted to get a feel for that method of body disposal. They knew the random dumping of strangled girls was a temporary disposal method.

I back away slowly, feeling an absentminded smile climb into my cheeks. *I've got you both now.*

I move, climbing over the short fence, and as I do, something inside begins to pull me, seemingly yanking me over the fence. An unseen force that fills me and makes me a bit clumsy in its sudden power. It reminds me of being in the alley with Stabber Brother and how my body split, part of me there and another directing me, watching me.

A surge of anticipation moves me across the manicured lawn, and it's only when I reach a window that I crouch and realize, other than my gloves, I have nothing on me. I left all my supplies in my Jeep. I take a second to look across the lot with all of its trees. The nearest house sits fifty or so yards away, with just as many trees on its lot.

I doubt anyone is watching, and if they were, they wouldn't see me through all this foliage. Still, though, I round the cottage to the back and completely out of sight.

A window sits low and staying crouched, I peer inside. It's a living room, normal enough, with nice fabric couches and a television. I keep going past the back door, around the small porch and come to the next window. It, too, sits low and the white blinds are shut tight.

I move a little bit, trying to find a spot in the blinds to see, and I line up with an inch gap where part of the blind is bent.

It's a bedroom, I note, and like the living room, normal enough with carpet, a dresser, and a bed. As I bring my hand up to shade the light and get a better view, a shadow inside shifts, and I freeze as a person crosses in front of the window.

But it's the back side of a person who doesn't even see me. I can't tell if it's Adam or Mr. Garner. The person keeps moving and now that I've got my hand up and can see better, I spy a body on the bed. But not just anybody, it's Adam, stripped to his underwear, unmoving.

For a few seconds, I myself don't move as I take in the scene. Long black leather straps wrap around his wrists and ankles, securing him to the bedposts. A purple ball gag has been lodged into his mouth and strapped around his head. A red satin scarf lays loose around his neck and I'm not sure if that means it's already been used or it's about to be used.

Adam's eyes sit open in an unnaturally wide way, and I narrow in on his stomach and the rapid shallow breaths. He's scared. He's not on that bed of his own free will.

His head rolls toward me almost like an unseen hand pushes it, as if he senses me at the window. Our gazes connect through the gap in the bent blind. There are many things in his eyes but the one that surfaces above all the rest is fear.

I see it now—through all the twists and turns—it's clear as day what Adam has been up to. He played on The Stranglers' obsession to lure them in, and now Adam is so far in he can't get out.

Mr. Garner steps back into view dressed in a black leather and mesh domination outfit, complete with a thong up his ass. His hair lays slicked back like he just wet it. His lean runner's body draws my attention with tan lines on his arm and legs, a pale chest, and no chest hair. He probably shaves it.

Adam's gaze jerks away from mine, and he flinches when he sees Mr. Strangler. He shows his teeth, and there's an edge of savage glee on his face. It makes the hair on my neck stand up. This will be the first kill he does without his wife. I know that look. I've had that look. Mr. Strangler likes control. He needs it, and I'm about to take it from him.

Time to bring this to an end. I slide away from the window and around to the back door. It's locked but a quick search for a hide-a-key and I find one in a magnetized box attached to the air conditioner unit. Using the key, I open the back door, and I step right inside.

I move silently through the house and into the bedroom. Mr. Strangler is over by a trunk now, smaller in size to the one we found in his condominium. The lid sits open, displaying the contents inside. I watch as he unzips a leather bag and pulls out several neatly rolled silk scarves. He goes about carefully laying them out—a green one, a blue one, a purple one, and a pink one—each monogrammed with the names of the strangled girls:

Caley, Zabrina, Evelyn, and Yasmin.

Those are his trophies, and the red one currently around Adam's neck is intended to join the others. Now that Mrs. Strangler is gone, Mister can move on from young girls to young boys. Oh, yes, I bet he's extremely excited about that one.

Adam squirms and makes a muffled sound, and Mr.

Strangler glances over. "I know. I know," he coos, oozing charm. "Don't be scared."

My gaze flicks off the scarfs and over to Adam to find his eyes locked on mine. They scream at me now with frantic madness. *What are you doing?* And he's right, what *am* I doing? I'm waiting for Mr. Strangler to see me. Coming up behind him is too easy. I want to see his eyes. I want, no, I *need* to play.

Adam's whole body begins violently quivering, and tears leak from the corners of his eyes. They trail down his face to plop onto the dark blue silk sheet.

Mr. Strangler lurches to his feet, finally sensing my presence, and when he turns, he freezes. For a moment, and without moving, he watches me with an unblinking stare that reminds me of a lizard.

"You know," I speak in a conversational tone. "Adam over there killed your wifey." I shrug. "Wasn't sure if you knew that or not. He put her in his trunk, and I cannot confirm or deny, but I'm pretty sure when he cremated her, she was still alive. Then I was the one who scooped up her ash and bones and delivered it to you in a box."

Mr. Strangler's brows come down in this confused way, and I'm not sure if it's because I'm standing here in the kill room starting a conversation with him, or if it's because he's digesting what I just said about his wife.

"I don't believe you," he whispers, and I find it odd that is how he chooses to respond to all of this.

I keep going with the conversation. "Oh, believe it. Kudos to you though for going to the cops. I was curious to see how you'd handle it. Smart move, then the cops think you're innocent. Though I know where you dumped your sex trunk. I followed you. Yes, we know all about you and Scott and Ted. We know about your little sex videos. What you probably don't know is that Ted is dead." I nod to Adam. "He killed Ted, too. So you've been framing a dead person."

Still, with the confused look, he glances between me and Adam. "Who are you two?"

"We're your judge and jury, and you are beyond guilty. Oh and P.S. I'm a firm believer in the death penalty."

Mr. Strangler takes a hesitant step back. "No, we didn't mean it. We didn't mean to kill anyone."

And there it is, the confession trapped people always seem to give. Do they think saying that they didn't mean it actually matters?

"It just happened," he nearly whines.

"And then it happened again, and again, and again. You're a killer and so was your wife. You're both monsters. Animals. You're the stuff of nightmares." I shift closer. "I'm going to kill you now," I tell him. I didn't come here with the intention of killing anyone. I came here just to see what was going on. But I like to think I'm flexible. I keep my options open. "What do you think about that?"

This animal is trapped, and trapped animals will chew off their own paw to get free. It's a survival instinct. Let's see what Mr. Strangler will do.

I watch him, standing there in his black leather and mesh dominating outfit. Not so dominating right now, though. He glances again to Adam, back to me, to Adam, and I almost laugh. He's trying to figure out how to get out of this.

I decide to make the decision for him. I lunge for him, and his face makes a satisfying crack when my knuckles connect. An unexpected jolt of pain vibrates through my shoulder, and I think I must have twisted it weird when I punched. I use that pain, though, to sharpen my focus as my entire world zeroes in on this man, this animal.

He's sluggish from my one punch, and though I see his coming, I let him make contact with me. I welcome it. He goes for my stomach, but he must really be dazed because it makes little impact. That or my adrenaline blocks it.

Mr. Strangler swings again, and I tilt back, barely registering the graze across my chin. But that graze seems to break through and my adrenaline kicks in full force. I grab him by the black leather straps crisscrossing his chest and I ram him into the wall. The mountainous scenic picture hanging there falls off its nail and onto the floor.

He yells something, but I don't hear it as I rear back and sink my fist into his stomach, delivering the type of punch he tried to.

Mr. Strangler curses and manages to get a good shove in, hard enough that I stumble back onto the bed and Adam. Whatever daze Mr. Strangler was in seems to have lifted, and he makes a dash for the door. I'm off the bed in no time, and I grab him and toss him across the room into the dresser.

With a groan, he rolls away and onto the floor, scampering into the corner. But I stalk him, and I drag him right back up. I want this killer stopped, but I'm not ready for him to be down yet. I want him to fight. I don't want things to end so soon.

He swings out, clocking me in the side of the head, surprising himself more than me, and the whole thing serves to only irritate me. But then his knee comes up, making contact with my ribs, and my whole body jerks with the pain.

I shove him hard, letting him know I'm the one in control, and his skull cracks against the wall. It's a hard crack and his head lists to the side as his body slides down to the floor. In this moment I know, I know, one more hit and he'll be out altogether.

But that's not what I want. I wrap my gloved fingers around his neck, and I squeeze, my muscles straining, my jaw clenching down. The Strangler's eyes pop wide, and I press harder, letting him feel every bit of pain he gave to his victims, letting him know his life is about to end.

Even if I wanted to, I can't stop now. The need to see his life end comes big and strong. For a second I fight it, more to see if I can than I really want to, but something growls inside of me like I'm a damn wolf during a full moon. I have to finish, I have to do this. This is happening.

Mr. Strangler gasps, he strains, his face contorts in agony, but none of it matters because I can't stop. I don't want to. My muscles strain, my fingers dig in stronger than I ever thought I could, like someone else is helping me.

A rising anger stampedes through me, thumping heavy at my organs, and a darkness crawls across my shoulders. It's not a gradual thing, like you see in the movies, his life slowly draining. No, it happens quickly—he's here with his bugged eyes and then he's not as his body goes slack.

Something pounds in my head, so loud I can't hear my own thoughts. I don't let go, I keep squeezing watching the blood vessels pop on his face and down his neck. I keep squeezing until I feel his neck pop. Until I break skin and blood seeps over my gloved fingers.

A viciousness rises up in me, traveling my spine and threading through me. I recognize it as the savage glee I saw earlier on this man's face. I fight against it. I won't be like him.

Behind me Adam thrashes on the bed, groaning.

The sound of him breaks the spell, and I release the grip I have on Mr. Strangler's neck.

I wipe my gloved fingers on my jeans and hurry over to the bed, but my skin still buzzes with the energy of the kill as I remove the ball gag from his mouth. Then I begin working on his wrists and ankles.

"Lane," Adam croaks, and his voice whips across me, bringing me completely back to the here and now and ridding my body of the odd energy that was buzzing through it seconds ago.

I look at him then, and his light brown eyes fill with fresh tears. I lay a calm hand on his shoulder, the same hand I just killed Mr. Strangler with. "It's okay," I assure him. "He's dead. You're safe."

60

DEATH. **IT EVOKES** a strong response. We all react in different ways to it. Some shed tears like when Dr. Issa died and Zach stood there and cried. Some turn to rituals like when Mom died and everyone brought us casseroles. Some rely on focus like with me and burying myself in my world.

Some also go through shock, as evidenced by Adam still on the bed. Though I've untied him, he sits curled up against the headboard in his underwear, his arms wrapped tightly around his bent knees. He won't stop shaking. Or babbling. "I-I...it happened so quickly. I thought I would get here, and go through the motions, and then make my move. B-but he had me completely helpless before I even knew it."

The fake mustache he was wearing earlier still sits glued above his upper lip. It's coming off on one corner, and I really want to rip it the rest of the way. He's in shock, and I don't know what to do.

"I-it was so easy with the wife." Adam's lashes blink several times, real quick. "I lied to them. I told them I helped Scott and Ted make the videos. It was an instant 'in' for me. I drugged the wife and put her in my trunk and-and-and it was so easy. B-but here." Adam sucks in a breath. "He was going to kill me. I was going to throw his body in the well and cover it with cement, and h-he was going to kill me."

Well, I guess that explains the cement I found in the trunk of Adam's car.

He doesn't say anything after that, and I leave him to his thoughts as I turn to stare down at Mr. Strangler. Now, what to do with the body. The well and cement idea isn't bad, but I have another idea.

"We should call our parents," Adam tells me. "Maybe it's time we let them in on everything we did."

I turn away from Mr. Strangler to look at Adam. "He was a cold-blooded killer and so was his wife. They both deserved what they got. If we make this official, it'll tear all of our lives apart. Do you really want that?"

"S-so we just keep this secret? Along with the others?" Adam shakes his head. "I'm beginning to hate secrets."

"We all have them."

"How am I supposed to go on? How am I supposed to live with everything I did? I've killed two people, Lane."

Well, three if you count the mercy-kill of his dad, but I don't think now is the time to point that out.

"You just do," I say. "You lashed out in anger when Scott died. You lost a brother, and you went after the whole world for it. It's understandable."

Adam's arms tighten around his knees. "My life was fine until you stepped into it."

I tilt back, not bothering to hide my shock. "*What*?"

He doesn't respond to my shock, and where I expect anger to flare in me, it doesn't and instead, I rationally say, "Fine like how? Like Scott and his sex videos? Or your alcoholic abusive dad? Or your mom who you claim barely knows you exist?"

Fresh tears fill his eyes. "What do you know about anything?"

"I know more than you think." It's right there on the tip of my tongue, my deepest darkest secret, ready to be told. I want Adam to know he's not alone with all of this.

"I-it was a lie. My father. I wasn't the one who ended his life. It was Scott. I stole the story from him to make me more interesting. He was always the brave one, protecting me from Dad. The funny one who could make Mom laugh. The good looking one who always had friends. He was everything, and I've never been anything."

This boy has lied to me so many times, and I didn't even know it. Somehow my reliable inner sense that tells me if someone is bullshit or not hasn't been so reliable with Adam. It's been more off than on. This should probably worry me, or make me angry, but it doesn't.

Maybe because I sense honesty in him that has never been there before. He's laying all his cards on the table. Or perhaps it's the lingering effects over the fact I killed his brother. Or it could be a very simple kindred thing. I feel responsible for him. We have an *emotional connection.*

"Adam, I know what it's like to feel like the odd man out, like something is off, like something is missing from your life. I know what it's like to be faced with the truth and it be ugly. I haven't had an easy year, but the one thing I have learned is that the sins of our family will go on and on unless someone, you or me, chooses a different path."

But is that what I'm doing, choosing a different path? Some days it feels like I am, others not. All I know is that it feels good to visit the other part of me, and as long as I keep it channeled in the right direction, I am choosing that different path.

Several long seconds tick by and slowly, he unwinds his arms from around his knees and slides to the edge of the bed. Gripping the side of the mattress, he lifts his gaze to mine, and I see something that wasn't there before—a peacefulness maybe, or more like acceptance. "I feel like an injured dog and you just removed my thorn."

Even though I like that analogy, it makes me chuckle. Sometimes Adam has the corniest thoughts.

He looks around the room. "What are we going to do?"

61

I RETRIEVED THE small bag of Ted's ash and bones that I kept just in case from my Jeep and placed it in the sex trunk. We wiped down anything Adam touched and stripped the bed. We left Mr. Strangler right where I killed him with all the evidence that linked him to Ted's death, the strangled girls, and his wife.

With it all, the D.A. got her justice for her son Scott's death and would never be faced with handing over the sex tapes.

We didn't call the body in, and it took a few days for it to be found. Of course, the whole thing hit the media as the story unraveled and played out exactly as I had hoped. No one knows for sure who killed Mr. Strangler, but some suspect it was a victim who got away. They'll search for the fictitious victim for a while, but eventually, that will die down too.

Now one week later, my phone rings, and it's Adam. "Hey," I greet him.

"Hey back."

"How you holding up?"

He sighs. "Did you see my mom on the news? All high and mighty and soaking in the media on this."

If I thought this was going to bring Adam and his mom closer together, I was wrong. The few times me and Adam have spoken over the week, things seem even more tense than usual in that department.

"Listen, I have some news," he goes on. "A few months ago before we even met, I applied to be an exchange student in China in one of their emerging technology programs. I found out yesterday I got it, and I'm going."

I think this is probably the best thing for him. Get out of the area and give him and his mom some space. Adam needs to find out who he really is without the ghosts of his dad and brother haunting him. Without the ghosts of Teddy and Mrs. Strangler, too. "I think that sounds fabulous," I tell him.

"Yeah, me too. I leave next week, and I was wondering, you're getting your own apartment soon, right? Will you consider taking Sally?"

I smile because that is about the best question ever. "I will definitely take Sally." Even if I am stuck in a dorm, I'll figure it out.

"Cool. We'll see each other before I leave."

"Sounds good." I click off, and for the first time in my entire friendship with Adam, I feel a sense of peace. We're at a place now we haven't been before. Our friendship evolved beyond the twists and turns, lies and manipulations into a place of trust and acceptance. I'm glad Adam came into my life. Sure he knows some of my secrets, but I know his, too.

And somehow I also know this isn't the end of mine and Adam's story.

"Lane!" Justin yells from downstairs. "Tommy's here!"

With a smile, I take the stairs down and find him already

sitting on the couch playing Legos with Justin. I look at the two of them with fondness as I slide in beside my boyfriend, slipping my arm around his middle and giving him a quick kiss on the cheek.

"Hey, where were you last night?" I ask.

He shrugs. "Had a few things to do."

Tommy's got his secrets, and I'm going to respect that. It only seems fair given everything I keep from him. Yes, we all have secrets and in that way I'm just like everyone else.

Kind of.

I settle back on the couch, idly watching my brother and my boyfriend play with Legos. In the kitchen, Victor is making homemade pizza and over at the dining room table, Daisy is clicking away on her laptop. I'm not sure if she and Hammond have made up or not, but I'll ask later.

Justin giggles at something Tommy says, and I smile. Yeah, life is pretty great. I'll hopefully have my own apartment soon and Sally, the dog. I'll be here local for my family. I'm going to be the best damn sister and daughter I can. And now I even have a boyfriend. I used to think I was hollow and empty inside, but I'm not.

How did all of this happen? Before I couldn't wait to leave and to be alone, but now I wouldn't want to be anywhere else. Is it because I want to belong? Is it because I want to be a part of something bigger than just me and my twisted legacy? Either way, I'm here.

But what do I really have to offer my family? It's just me here, demented Lane. But who's perfect? Certainly not me. The question is, what happens next?

For the first time in my life, I don't care. I'm content, and I'm here in this moment. I'm happy. Yes, life is good.

A rattling bag draws my attention over to Daisy at the

dining room table. She's pulling a box from a paper bag and it's the giant initials DNA that makes me sit up.

"What are you doing?" The words leave my mouth before I can stop them, and they must leave my mouth in a loud tone because every single person stops what they're doing to look at me.

Daisy hesitates. "Um, one of those Ancestry DNA tests everyone's been doing lately."

I steal a glance at Victor as I get up from the couch and walk straight over to her. I lower my voice, looking at her long and hard. "I don't want you to do that."

Her voice is soft and weak, when she says, "I already did."

Read the next book in the series:

The Suicide Killer

ACKNOWLEDEMENTS

Novels do not get written in a vacuum. It is a team effort for sure! I want to first thank Patrick Price, my editor. He fell in love with Lane from the beginning and has been an ongoing cheerleader for her vigilante ways.

I'd also like to thank Steven at Novak Illustration for the excellent exterior design.

My readers, too, who are the sole reason why I write stories. Thank you for your support!

To the team of beta readers of *The Strangler* who offered invaluable input and enthusiasm. In alphabetical order: Teresa Beasley, Brandi Brinkley, Madison Burkett, Megan Forno, Kayla Gilbert, Sabrina Klotz, Cloé Lalonde-LeBlond, Dora Landa, T. Lucas, L. Michelle Medone, Charley Meredew, Elizabeth J. Miller, Kelsey Miller, Nicolle Pizarro, Jessica Porter, Kaitlyn Puckett, Freya Schalla, Tristan Shirley, Keisha Smith, Paige Ulevich.

To Karin Perry for creating fabulous swag. You can check her store out on Zazzle under Doodle_with_Karin

ABOUT THE AUTHOR

Things you should know about me: I write novels. Some have won awards. Others have been bestsellers. Under Shannon Greenland (my real name) you'll find spies, adventure, and romantic suspense. Under S. E. Green (my pen) you'll find dark and gritty fiction about serial killers, cults, secret societies that do bad things, and whatever else my twisted brain deems to dream up.

I'm on Instagram, Twitter, and Facebook. I can also be found at www.segreen.net. There you can sign up for my newsletter where you can keep up to date with new releases, free stuff (like books), and my mild ramblings about my travels. I have a very old and grouchy dog. But I love him. My humor runs dark and so don't be offended by something off I might say. I mean no harm. I live in a small Florida beach town but I'm most often found exploring the world. I eat entirely too many chips. I also love math!

. . .

Turn the page for a complete list of books!

Did you know reviews are important?
They help authors sell books and readers find those books.
Please consider leaving one!

BOOKS BY S. E. GREEN

Monster

When the police need to crawl inside the mind of a monster, they call Caroline. It takes a survivor to know a madman...

Vanquished

A secret island. A sadistic society. And the woman who defies all odds to bring it down.

Ultimate Sacrifice

A murdered child. A small town. A cult lurking in the shadows...

Twisted Truth Box Set

Includes four bestselling, award-winning novels. Its pages full of visceral and provocative, raw and gritty, heart-pumping, edge-of-your-seat reads.

BOOKS BY SHANNON GREENLAND

The Specialists Series

The Summer My Life Began Series

Made in the USA
Middletown, DE
15 November 2020